Daughters
of the
House

Daughters
of the
House

MICHÈLE ROBERTS

OTHER WORKS BY MICHÈLE ROBERTS

FICTION
A Piece of the Night
The Visitation
The Wild Girl
The Book of Mrs Noah
In the Red Kitchen

POETRY
The Mirror of the Mother
Psyche and the Hurricane

FILM
The Heavenly Twins

PLAYS
The Journeywoman

*She has also co-authored four books of poetry
and four collections of short stories*

Published by VIRAGO PRESS Limited 1992
20–23 Mandela Street, Camden Town, London NW1 0HQ

A CIP catalogue record for this book
is available from the British Library

Typeset by Falcon Typographic Art Ltd, Fife, Scotland
Printed in Great Britain

ISBN 1 85381 550 0

Author's Note

A major source of inspiration for this novel was *L'histoire d'une âme* by Thérèse Martin, who is more often known as Saint Thérèse of the Child Jesus, also as The Little Flower. Just as my Thérèse is a fictional character, so the village of Blémont-la-Fontaine is an imaginary one, its inhabitants existing only on paper.

My thanks to Caroline Dawnay, Lennie Goodings, Jim Latter and Elsbeth Lindner for reading and criticizing earlier drafts of this novel.

for Beewee

THE WALL

*I*t was a changeable house. Sometimes it felt safe as a church, and sometimes it shivered then cracked apart.

A sloping blue slate roof held it down. Turrets at the four corners wore pointed blue hats. The many eyes of the house were blinded by white shutters.

What bounded the house was skin. A wall of gristle a soldier could tear open with his bare hands. Antoinette laughed. She was buried in the cellar under a heap of sand. Her mouth was stuffed full of torn-up letters and broken glass but she was tunnelling her way out like a mole. Her mouth bled from the corners. She laughed a guttural laugh, a Nazi laugh.

The house was strict. The rules indicated the forbidden places. Chief of these was the bedroom at the back on the first floor, at the top of the kitchen stairs.

The rules said you mustn't go there. It was for your own protection. Each time Léonie tried she had to halt. The terror was so strong. It pushed her away, wouldn't let her come near. Behind the terror was something evil which stank and snarled and wanted to fix her in its embrace. Better to flee, to clatter back across the bare plank floor of the landing, find the headlong stairs and fall down them. Better to stay at the front of the house.

Antoinette was dead, which was why they had buried her in the cellar. She moved under the heap of sand. She clutched her red handbag, which was full of shreds of dead flesh. She was trying to get out, to hang two red petticoats on the washing-line in the orchard. Sooner or later she would batter down the cellar door and burst up through it on her dead and bleeding feet.

The deadness and the evil and the stink were inside Léonie. She rushed up the cellar steps, magically she erupted into her own bed in the dark, the smell of warm blood, soaked sawdust.

Now she was properly awake. She ran to the bathroom to be sick. It was Thérèse she was throwing up. She vomited her forth, desperate to be rid of her and then weak with gasping relief that she was gone.

THE WRITING-TABLE

*L*éonie was waiting for Thérèse to arrive. She longed for her, like a lover. Her mind bristled with knives. She imagined the edge of the blade, silvery and saw-toothed. Its tip vanishing into Thérèse's soft flesh.

She could not settle. She paced up and down the corridor in which things had stood in their places since long before she was born. The little buttoned armchair in worn pink brocade. The two porcelain jars, plump dragons, that guarded the writing-table. The mirror with its broken-pediment frame. The strip of silk carpet, bald in places, frayed.

These items her eyes checked one by one. They were hers. As the house was. Hers to dispose of as she wished and thought proper. She would not share them with Thérèse. She had cared for the house, spent her money on it, kept it in good repair. All these years of tending it meant that it was hers.

This morning she had begun listing the house contents in the inventory her lawyer had suggested she draw up. But she was too excited to go on. She would continue with her task once Thérèse had arrived and settled in. She wondered how long she ought to wait before asking Thérèse about her plans. She promised herself to be very tactful, very discreet.

The writing-table stood against the wall, facing it, halfway down the corridor which ran, on the first floor, along the back of the house. Antoinette, in the days when she was well enough, had sat here to write notes of invitation, letters to her sisters. Madeleine, and then Léonie, had gone on using her pen, blue ink, leather-bound blotter. Léonie perched here, on the curvy-backed chair with a tapestry seat, to do her accounts. And now the inventory.

The mirror opposite her flickered a warning. Which of us is which? For twenty years she had cohabited peacefully with her reflection, peering at it to check that she'd got what she thought she'd got. Yes, she existed, the mirror told her over those years: with her smooth surface, fresh gilding, only a little tarnish. Now that other one was turning up, to disrupt her steady gaze.

When she looked at Thérèse, what would she see? She supposed they had both aged. If she smashed her fist into Thérèse's face, would she hear the crack and splinter of glass? She wondered whether Thérèse's sheltered life had kept her looking young. When they were both sixteen she had been pleased to make comparisons. She had better legs than Thérèse, a sharper clothes sense, a more fashionably slender body. When Thérèse arrived she would be able to carry on that old war.

Up and down she paced. She liked the sound of her footsteps measuring the long silence of the corridor. As she liked the fact that the corridor had doors at both ends, represented both pause and process. Was not a room but was between rooms. Both connected and separated them.

When you came up the curve of the oval staircase on to the first floor, you arrived in a hallway set with doors half-concealed in grey panelling. Opening the furthest on the left, you passed into a second, tiny, hall, off which opened Antoinette's old bedroom and the bathroom. A third grey-painted door, part of the panelling like all the others, led out of this little lobby into the corridor.

Thérèse would remember which door was which. She would not arrive, as Léonie still did in her dreams, as a stranger, confused by the labyrinth that was the house, discovering the corridor at the back as a surprise. Thérèse would walk into the house as her birthright, the place she'd lived in all through her childhood. She would see Léonie as the usurper, Léonie as the one who stole what was not hers to inherit. Thérèse the prodigal would return wanting everything.

Would Thérèse remember the room at the other end of the corridor, and what it had once held? Did she ever dream of trying to walk into it in the dark? Did she ever wake, in a thrash of sweat, trembling and clenched, in her bed that for twenty years had been safely foreign and far away?

Léonie found that she was downstairs, in the centre of the kitchen. A rack of knives hung on the wall near the hood of the fireplace. Symmetry of thick black handles implanted with thin blades, razor fine. In English, she remembered explaining to Thérèse once: *wicked* could mean *sharp*. There was a gap in the row of knives. Léonie looked down, puzzled, at her hands. She discovered she was testing the tip of the vegetable knife, the ancient one with the ragged edge, against her thumb. She raised it. She divided the air in two. Then she let the knife drop on to the kitchen table.

She felt dizzy. As though Thérèse were already here and they were children again, playing that game of spinning on one spot with arms outstretched, seeing who could twirl longest and not fall.

THE DOORBELL

*T*hérèse arrived by bus. She insisted that she did not want to be met. I'm quite capable of walking, she told Léonie over the phone: I've still got the use of my legs, you know, and my brain, I haven't forgotten the way.

No scenes in public, was what she meant. Not that she expected Léonie to fall on her neck and call for the fatted calf to be slain. But she felt raw, as though she'd been flayed, all her old customs and gestures stripped off along with the brown dress she'd worn for twenty years. She didn't want to stand out, or be recognized. She would slink into the village anonymous and discreet. She would cover her face until she was ready to show it. She asked Léonie not to tell people she was coming back. No fuss. Let them find out in the ordinary course of things. To herself she added: when I've decided exactly what it is I must do.

The bus plunged along the banks of the Seine. Thérèse remembered strings of ancient houses, black and cream displays of timbering, plaster, thatch. The great flat river sliding between cliffs. A calm green emptiness which turned in spring to a pink carnival of flowering orchards. How many new houses there were now, how very tidy and rebuilt everything seemed. *Restored*, that was the word one used. *Corrected. Freshened.*

She felt peculiar. It was her clothes, she decided. Her knees exposed by the skirt of her dress riding up when she sat down. Her legs, nude in fawn nylons. Her general sense of skimpy coverings, of being too visible. In the bus she was a focus for others' glances, however casual, and she resented it.

When at Caudebec a couple of Algerian men got on to the bus Thérèse stared at them. Black people didn't live in the green

Norman countryside. Surely they all lived in ghettoes on the outskirts of cities.

Mutters from the other passengers reached her.

A bad lot, I'm afraid, always looking for trouble.

Far too many of them coming in.

Thérèse turned her head aside and gazed out of the window. Billboards hoisted posters in Gothic lettering that advertised ancient inns, traditional cider and Calvados, authentic butter and cheese. Grandmother's this and that, everything from pine furniture to apricot jam. The signs all pointed somewhere else: over there; that's the real thing. Then the bus jolted around a sharp corner with a blare of its horn and they swept into Blémont's little main street.

The bus-stop, just as in the old days, was the area of pavement outside the *Mairie*. This florid building was now painted salmon pink, no longer the faded grey that Thérèse remembered. She shrugged, watching the bus depart, backside of blue glass farting exhaust. She stooped to pick up her bags.

At the top of the street behind her was the village church. Beyond it, the cemetery, and the family grave. Her mother was buried there under a slab of polished granite, and her father, and his second wife Madeleine. In a far corner, separated from the fields beyond by a high wall, was the grave of Henri Taillé. His bones had been found eventually and brought here, and the tangle of bones of the unknown Jews buried with him. The shallow pit had opened and given them up. She wondered whether she should go there now, to see for herself what she had read about in the newspaper. The grave newly opened and desecrated, swastikas in red daubed on the tombstone. The church bells tolling gently decided her. She didn't want to be seen by the people turning out for early-evening Mass. She'd visit the cemetery in the morning. She would go very early, before anyone was about, and check the evidence with her own eyes.

She crossed the road, to take the turning that led off between the chemist's and the blacksmith's. Oh. There was no longer a blacksmith's. And the chemist's window, which used to contain antique apothecary pots in *vieux Rouen* porcelain, was now full of strip-lit placards of naked women scrubbing their thighs with green mittens. What was cellulite? Thérèse walked on.

She told herself that she was calm. That she was on the right road. That her feet did recognize its bends and loops. There was a pavement now, streetlamps and bus-shelters on this stretch, signs warning of sharp corners, an old people's home. The old school had been knocked down and a new one, prefab style, built in its place, next to an asphalt playground. Only half a kilometre on did the countryside as she remembered it burst upon her. She smelled grass, wet earth, manure. She saw tall poplars and beech trees flicker like feathers as the wind stirred them. She recognized the profiles of familiar barns.

The tall white wrought-iron gates stood open. Beyond them the little white manor-house floated in its courtyard of white gravel. The long lawn at one side was still surrounded by beds of silvery and white flowers. The massive cedar at its far end still looked like part of a stage-set. Thérèse gripped her bags more firmly and went forward.

Even though it was late afternoon there were no lights on in the house. Everything was still. As though Léonie had gone away. The windows did not blaze yellow as Thérèse wanted them to, did not burn, flags of welcome to herself, weary traveller, sister returning from exile. She trod across the gravel and pressed the white enamel doorbell under the little wrought-iron and glass porch. Light came on behind the long glass panels of the door. Someone wrenched it open from inside. It scraped and squeaked on the tiled floor of the hall, just as it always had. A woman with angry eyes under a shining fringe peered out. It was Léonie.

THE CHANDELIER

*T*he chandelier was made of metal twisted into leaves painted pale green. These twined about sprays of flowers, red stars with yellow hearts. Nestling in this hard wreath were improbable fruits, lemon-coloured globes of glass. The chandelier hung from one of the white iron struts that crisscrossed, in arches, the roof of the little conservatory at the back of the house. Thérèse, coming into it, was reminded of the railway station where she had broken her journey earlier that day: the draughty cold, the glass-and-metal-domed roof, the shadowy corners. Then Léonie, beside her, put out a hand and depressed a switch and the circlet of glass lemons dangling above their heads sprang into vibrant colour, gleamed out in yellow.

Chill struck up into Thérèse's feet from the grey tiles, speckled with red, that she stood on. Cold prickled inside her nose, around her neck and wrists. She tucked her hands into the sleeves of her cardigan, regretting having let Léonie take her coat. Why did Léonie choose to sit here of all places? Shivering, she looked about. The old wicker armchairs, their red and black paint almost completely worn off, still surrounded the wicker table. Scarlet and pink geraniums were rampant on all sides, just as they used to be. She snuffed up their rough fragrance. What was new was the plethora of vases, standing on every available surface, stuffed with sheaves of wheat, oats and barley. Someone had been busy transforming some of these into corn plaits and twists, which hung from the shelves supporting the geranium pots. The straw stalks were pale and glossy, woven into their ridged patterns by an obviously expert hand. Had Léonie taken up making corn dollies?

Light from the chandelier fell on Léonie's fair hair, two walls of satin that dropped exactly to jaw level. She wore black linen trousers, a brown silk polo-neck, expensively narrow shoes. Léonie was nearly forty, her blue eyes nested in crow's-feet and wrinkles, and she was a lot plumper than formerly. But there was something childish about her that made her seem younger than she was. Good skin, thought Thérèse: good legs. Why does that matter so much?

It always had. The right body, right clothes, right way of talking, of attracting and pleasing others: Thérèse hadn't had it. No, she thought: something much deeper, inside, that I felt I lacked, I didn't know what it was. Femininity? Not a real woman like the others? Had Léonie ever felt that?

She felt Léonie's eyes scamper over her. Now she would have to compete. She couldn't bear Léonie to see her in these ugly clothes she'd been given to come home in. Pale blue synthetic-stuff dress with ill-matching blue cardigan, navy court shoes that pinched. She wrapped her arms around herself and glared at a corn wreath twined with gold ribbon.

Oh those, Léonie chattered with a wave of her hand: leftover decorations for the harvest festival. It's tomorrow. I told you the date in my letter, remember? You'll see tomorrow, in church, the decorations are wonderful. Baptiste thinks it's important to keep up the old crafts. He says we mustn't let the old Norman traditions die out. You of all people should agree with that.

Thérèse shrugged, not knowing what to reply. She felt rusty. Not used to sociability. She glanced upwards for inspiration.

I'm glad you've still got the chandelier, she said: I remember when Papa put that up. He brought it back from Italy, he and Maman.

Of course I've still got it, Léonie said: why on earth would I want to get rid of it? Everything in this house that's old, that belonged to our family, is precious to me. I'd never get rid of anything.

So much anger prickled in the air between them that they took a step away from each other. Thérèse's feet fizzed. There was a tremor in her knees.

In a hurry Léonie said: Let's have a drink. We'll have supper later. I'll go and get some ice. Will you fetch the bottle and glasses? You know where they're kept. You know where the *buffet* is.

THE BUFFET

The clock had not changed. Its tick was the heavy heartbeat of the house, slow, the fall of metal brushes. It had measured out Thérèse's childhood. Moment after moment of endless afternoons. She'd forgotten it. Now, after twenty years, she heard it again.

The *buffet* stood in its old place opposite the clock. In one corner of the white-panelled dining-room, between the window, hung with frilled muslin, and the door out into the hall. The door-handle was a china egg, cold in her palm. Loose, it still wobbled, exactly as it used to. The door rattled, just as it had always done.

A local craftsman had made the *buffet* for the wedding of Thérèse's grandparents. It would have been hers if she had married. A solid piece in worn pine, darkened with age, satin-smooth. Its top pair of doors was carved with reliefs of oakleaf garlands. Two fat swags that hung down, one on each door. To open the *buffet* you didn't bother tugging at the key but instead inserted your finger into a silky hole at the base of one of the doors, and pulled.

Inside, on the top shelf, was the old arrangement of bottles of cassis, Bénédictine, Calvados and rum, glass flasks of oil and vinegar, blue pots of salt and mustard. On the middle shelf, just as before, were rows of wine and water glasses, stacks of dessert plates. On the bottom shelf lay neatly folded napkins and tablecloths. The napkin-cases laboriously embroidered by Thérèse and Léonie long ago, wobbly red cross-stitch on blue checked gingham, were still there.

Thérèse could not stop shivering. Thrifty Léonie had denied the cold in the house. It's only September. Far too early in the season to switch on the heating. So Antoinette's early training had held good with this most unlikely of candidates. Deny the body's needs and advance in holiness. Then Thérèse felt ashamed. Probably Léonie *was* hard up, running a house this size and with all those children to bring up. Who am I to criticize? Thérèse thought: for twenty years I haven't earned my own living, for twenty years I've been able to be irresponsible as a child.

She spotted a small woollen blanket padding one of the chairs drawn up to the dining-table. She picked it up, wrapped it about her shoulders. It smelled strongly of cat but she was too cold and tired to care. She took two glasses and a bottle of gin from the *buffet*, put them on the tray she found on a nearby side-table. A wizened lemon lurked in a glass bowl. But no tonic. She would have to go and see whether it was kept in the kitchen. Don't rush, she told herself: it's only your first alcoholic drink in twenty years.

She went the long way round. Deliberately chose to take a detour, so that she could make a quick check on the house and on her memories of it. See whether Léonie had hung hideous examples of craft work all over the place or moved the furniture about. She tiptoed through all the rooms on the ground floor, lighting them one by one as she opened their doors then plunged through them and left them behind her in the dark again. Fragrance of potpourri in some places, of furniture polish, of cats, of dust. More corn dollies. Fussy arrangements of dried flowers. Modern children's litter of tennis rackets, records, board games. Curved tunnel of rooms, one leading out of, into, another. Thérèse forgot her wish to inspect for changes, instead fell into wonder.

Léonie could choose to sit in any one of three *salons*, small medium big, or in the conservatory. More rooms upstairs, on two floors. How dared she have so much choice, so much freedom of movement? Thérèse remembered the bare cell she had left behind her, the half-hour daily allotted to exercise. Dully walking up and down between two brick walls. In this house you could stride.

In the old days she had not noticed its size. It was home, and it was full of people. Her child's eye had not been overwhelmed by these chilly mausoleums Antoinette called sitting-rooms, had created the spaces she needed, her own small ones she could pull round her. Tonight she was unsure of her size as she blundered through the dark. She stumbled on a stone step and fell into the kitchen.

It was just as she remembered it. A large square room dominated by its blackleaded range. Wooden table, carved dresser stacked with bowls and plates. The wall of the chimney breast above the range, and the wall above the marble shelf where the eggs were still kept, she was pleased to see, in a wire basket, were decorated with old blue and white tiles. The kitchen was dark. Blackened. That was how she'd seen it as a child. A cave, in whose shadowy corners swam blue figures on a cream ground, the gleam and streak of marble. Now a modern cooker squeezed in next to the range. A new fridge, bright white, jutted behind the back door. Smart white spotlights wreathed their plastic necks above the table and cooker. Sensible enough, Thérèse supposed, and doubtless Victorine would have approved. At the moment the kitchen was lit by two candles set in flowered china candlesticks in front of the little plaster Virgin on a bracket on the wall. Others of Victorine's household gods remained too. The tin picture of a vase of roses nailed above the fridge. The white linen drying-up cloths, with a single red stripe, hung from the side of the sink. The wooden plate-rack above the draining-board. The shallow wicker basket of red onions that stood next to the eggs on the marble shelf. If she ignored the cooker and the fridge then hardly anything had changed. Too much attachment to objects, she scolded herself. She had spent twenty years trying to practise detachment and she had failed. She'd discovered that as soon as she had re-entered the house.

My house, Thérèse corrected herself softly: *my* house. All of it.

She opened the fridge and took out the bottle of tonic.

THE BED

The tablecloth was thick, smooth and blue. Heavy Indian cotton, a thin turquoise line through blue checks. Small frayed holes here and there. Thérèse remembered pushing bored fingers through those openings, to enlarge them. Lunches in childhood had gone on so long.

Léonie insisted on laying the table properly, even though they were only going to eat in the kitchen. She twitched the cloth so that it hung evenly, flattened its rumples with a brisk hand. No excuse for being sloppy, things need to be done right. Thérèse could hear Victorine's monitoring voice as though she were in the room. Her heart unlocked and let out sayings she didn't know she'd stored.

She sat with her back pressed against the white metal pleats of the radiator. On the sidelines of this busy kitchen life. Wanting just to observe. She fiddled with her glass, sipped from it. Sparkly sweetness of gin and tonic, quinine, on her tongue. She felt twirled about, giddy. Drinking too fast.

Léonie put a rustic brown pottery jug, full of water, on the table. Its glaze was silvery. Zigzags had been cut in the clay before firing. She flanked it with an open bottle of red wine, the two flowered candlesticks from the bracket on the wall. One white candle and one cream-coloured. Their flames danced then steadied, climbing yellow about the sturdy black wicks. Two dark primrose soup plates in thick porcelain with wide fluted edges. Big silver soup spoons, silver forks, black-handled knives. The old cutlery Thérèse remembered. Placed by Léonie just so. A basket of chopped bread. Shining red pot of leek and potato soup with cream poured in. Hunger growled in her like a dog. She pulled up her chair to the table. Léonie sat opposite. In the calm golden glow of the candles they ate.

Soup just like Victorine used to make, Léonie said: of course. I use all her old recipes.

You think you've laid a real French supper, Thérèse thought: but you haven't got it quite right. I know that. But you don't. You grew up in England, don't forget. You with your peasant-style pots and your corn dollies. If she were alive Victorine would laugh at you.

She could only pick at her slice of roast veal in rich gravy.

I'm sorry, she apologized: I'm not used to such good food. Back there we always ate so simply.

She heard herself sounding priggish, felt herself flush. She watched Léonie reach for more *petits pois* and veal.

I'm too greedy I expect, Léonie said: food matters to me too much probably.

She pointed with her fork at Thérèse.

But you're so thin. Just skin and bone. Are you ill?

She doesn't want me to look good, Thérèse thought: slimmer than she is. Easier to see me as a burden, a sick person she'll have to look after, she's worried she'll never get me off her hands.

Eating sensibly, she declared: is crucial for health, a well-balanced diet and not too much of anything that's my motto.

Léonie laughed unwillingly over her heaped plate: Thérèse had imitated Victorine's voice and manner so precisely. But she was obviously angry: her gifts rejected, her control waved aside. Thérèse sat back, pleased with herself. Pleased too with her flat stomach, lean hips. No longer the fat girl she'd been as an adolescent. Her body obeyed her now. She watched Léonie mop her plate with a piece of bread and eat it with relish, pour herself more wine. Léonie used to be skinny as a boy. No one could call her too thin these days, that was certain.

She finally remembered to ask.

How's Baptiste? Where is he tonight? And where are the girls? Have you drowned them all three or what?

Baptiste's got a meeting in the village, Léonie said: you remember, he's the mayor now, I did write and tell you. And the girls, they're scattered all over the place. Summer camp. Staying with friends. Travelling. The house is so quiet, I feel like a ghost in it.

They did kiss each other good night. As they had kissed on meeting. A brushing of cheeks, the lips kept well away from contact with skin. Léonie's obvious excuse being that she had thick red lipstick on. She used to ask Thérèse for kisses: a real big smacker that's what I want. Pain woke and stretched inside Thérèse.

She said: I'm so tired, I must go to bed, we'll have a proper chat tomorrow won't we.

Of course, Léonie said.

Thérèse picked up the larger of her two bags from where Léonie had dumped them earlier in the hall. She started up the stairs with it. Her body sagged with fatigue.

Don't worry about the other one, Léonie called up after her: I'll bring it up for you later on.

Don't bother, Thérèse said: I don't need it. Not tonight anyway.

Léonie had given Thérèse the best bedroom. The one that the Martin parents used to sleep in together before Antoinette moved to the smaller one next door, nearer the bathroom. Louis had gone on sleeping in this one, alone. Then later on he had moved downstairs. Thérèse wondered a little at Léonie's choice of room to offer her. Tomorrow she would pick at motives, admitted and secret. Tonight she was merely relieved that her fingers knew exactly where to find the round end of the light-switch just inside the door. Where the hand-basin hid behind a faded blue curtain. How to unhook the fastenings of the little white cupboards on either side of the oblong sink.

His things. All these years after his death they were still here. Zipped brown leather case containing silver-backed brushes and silver-topped bottles. White china seashell embracing Roget Gallet tea-rose soap. Folded linen towels for face and hands. The room was a shrine, relics lovingly preserved. Intact. Dusted, washed, ironed. By Léonie? Thérèse's feet slipped her away, over the embroidered cotton rugs, towards the bed.

This stood in the far corner opposite the door, its mattress fitted into a mahogany frame curved and scrolled at top and bottom. Next to it was a little marble-topped stand bearing a lamp, a fluted green glass with a white rose in it. Under the glass was a square white cloth with a lace edge, starched, glossily flat.

Thérèse sank into plumy depths. The mattress was as cushiony as the quilt encased in red silk, the pillow large and square. Bedding luxurious as cream.

The wallpaper was still the same. A design of tiny sprigs of pink and cream roses on what had been once, Thérèse remembered, a brilliant blue background and was faded now to a pleasing indigo. She stared at the crucifix which hung on the wall opposite her, at the slender switch of palm tucked behind the ivory Christ. Her hands went up to check the cotton scarf she had tied around her head.

She'd been born in this bed. She rolled over, she felt she must, to make space for her mother beside her, newly delivered after a day and a night of labour.

THE HOLDALL

*L*éonie waited half an hour, until she was sure Thérèse must be asleep. She balanced outside her bedroom door, breath hushed and ears cocked. No sound. No halo of light between door and frame.

She glided back downstairs. She'd seen Thérèse's look travel scornfully over her plumpness, oh yes, but at least she was still light on her feet. She made a good spy. Now she needed to hurry. Before Baptiste got home. She didn't want him to catch her rifling through Thérèse's things.

She picked up the holdall from where Thérèse had left it at the bottom of the stairs and took it into the kitchen. Pushing aside the debris of supper things she dumped it on the table. She shook her head at it. Ugly and cheap, like the clothes Thérèse had arrived home in. Blue plastic, with a worn strap. She told herself she was justified in looking inside. To keep one step ahead in this uneasy game.

It wasn't locked. So it wasn't private, really. And leaving it around was just asking for someone to open it. She tugged the zip past places where it stuck, wrenched the bag's mouth apart. Words were inside. Books. She lifted them out. Paperbacks mainly. Modern French history. Jewish history. Léonie's fingers came up to pull at her lower lip.

Underneath the volumes of history, at the bottom of the holdall, was a notebook. Pages covered in Thérèse's well-behaved rounded script. She wrote in blue ballpoint, a cheap one that left thick blue blots. Léonie's own name cropped up quite a lot. Stuff about their childhood.

Léonie flicked over the leaves of squared paper, then turned back to the first page. Thérèse had written her title with flourishes, had underlined it three times. *The story of a soul.* Léonie grimaced. Presumably Thérèse was now an expert in such matters.

Léonie went to Mass every Sunday with her husband and children. It was what you did, like going to school, going to the clinic to give birth. What she liked best about Sundays was going to the baker's afterwards to buy cakes for lunch, then coming home to hot chocolate and a slice of *galette*, sipping her *apéritif* while relishing the smell of roast lamb from the kitchen.

Thérèse had listed words like *soul, God, sin, miracle, prayer.* Léonie's inventory sang a litany of beds and tables and chairs. I haven't got a soul, have I, she thought: Thérèse stole it.

THE GREY SILK
NIGHTSHIRT

*T*hérèse yawned into her pillow. A silky bag of feathers held in a linen envelope. Too big and fat. There was too much of everything in this house. Too much food, too much drink, too much noise. She had heard Léonie come to her door, stand there listening, go away again. She had heard Baptiste arrive home, car tyres scattering the gravel and the dog she hadn't met yet waking up in its kennel to bark. She had heard the front door scrape open, just under her window, Léonie's cheerful voice shouting hush, make that dog be quiet, don't wake Thérèse. Ten minutes or so ago she had heard them come upstairs together, an exaggeratedly quiet progress towards bed, caricature of tiptoe walking. What was Baptiste like to make love with? Years ago, she could admit it now: she had been tempted to find out. But then God had grabbed her and after that it was too late.

Baptiste despised her. That's what he had told Léonie all those years ago, that day when Thérèse had spied on them in the woods. She had listened to them and she had watched them. Their white legs. Then she had run off to fetch the priest.

She gave up trying to sleep, rolled over and switched on the lamp by the bed. She sat up and smoothed her fingers over the creases in her face. Even before she heard the hand fumbling at the door-handle she knew who was there. They'd always been able to pick up each other's presence. That day in the woods Léonie had known. She'd chosen her audience. She'd waited until she was sure Thérèse had arrived and was hidden behind the trees.

The door clicked open then shut. Léonie had on a grey silk nightshirt, with white piping, that just failed to cover her knees. Much fatter than they used to be, Thérèse noticed. She had a cigarette in one hand and puffed on it before she spoke. She waved it at Thérèse.

D'you mind?

Thérèse shrugged.

Not if you don't, I suppose.

Léonie's face shone with cold cream. Slabs of it laid on above her cheekbones, filling in the wrinkles like plaster of Paris. Her eyes glared through this glistening mask of white. She came across the room, picking up an ashtray on the way, and perched on the end of Thérèse's bed. She drew her legs up under her and rested her weight on one hand.

I forgot to ask you earlier on, d'you want to borrow something to wear to church tomorrow morning? I wasn't sure what clothes you've brought with you. You won't need a hat of course.

Thérèse moved against the pillow propping her back. She put up a hand to touch the scarf that wrapped her head. The nearness of Léonie's nightshirt, gleaming and loose, decided her. She pulled off the headscarf and dropped it on the quilt. She ran her fingers through her chopped hair.

Yes, she said: thanks, that might be a good idea.

The crumpled bit of cotton was blue as Léonie's tobacco smoke which hung in the air in wisps. Blue as the wallpaper behind her. Léonie looked at Thérèse's semi-scalped head. She took a deep drag of her cigarette, coughed, blinked. She screwed up her eyes, which were watering. She pointed. Thérèse reached out and switched off the bedside lamp.

Léonie said: tell me why you've come back. You've stood the life there for twenty years, why d'you suddenly want a break from it now? I don't believe what you said in your letter. You're not here for a holiday. You're up to something. Tell me what it is.

Thérèse thought: in the darkness we're equal. One married and one not, one plump and one thin, one truthful and one a liar, one who belongs and one who doesn't. It doesn't matter any more, our difference. It's all flattened out. Like wearing the habit. No bodies you have to notice. Freedom. Sisters together under the skin, made identical.

She smoothed out the headscarf and laid her hands neatly on top of it. She instructed them not to get excited and wave about. Léonie was a hump of darkness at the other end of the bed, crouched over a burning red dot. The dot lengthened, fell.

We used to sit up like this when we were young, didn't we? Thérèse said: talking. We used to tell each other everything. All our secrets.

Did we? Léonie said.

Her silky bulk rolled nearer Thérèse. She smelled of facecream and flowery scent and cigarettes. She wriggled her shoulders, shifted her legs, put one hand back under her head. With the other she stubbed out her cigarette on the invisible ashtray balanced on the dark bump of her stomach. She waited. She was at home. Thérèse thought: I haven't, I chose not to, for all those years, I had forgotten.

The pleasure of two heads, close, turned towards each other in the dark. Whispers. Certain confidences could be exchanged only in the friendly night. When you were unembarrassed, more honest. When you couldn't clearly see the other's face but knew, from the tilt of her head, that she was listening. Her mouth and warm breath nearby.

Thérèse had taken a vow of poverty all those years ago. She had chosen silence. She had stripped off language like gold necklaces, pearl rings. She had few words ready for use now. She picked some out of her meagre hoard, tossed them like jacks in her palm, threw some back.

As far as the convent's concerned I'm here on a visit to my family. We're allowed out for short holidays now you know. It's just that I never chose to take one before. I thought I'd never want to come back.

Léonie sighed. She fished in her nightshirt pocket, fumbled with her packet of cigarettes, her lighter.

I think I'm going to leave, Thérèse went on: but I haven't said anything yet.

Why? Léonie asked.

She lit a fresh cigarette and drew on it.

Thérèse lay back, limbs suddenly slack. She breathed in the smell of Léonie's body, her tobacco, her sweat. A good smell. Like that of Louis. The traces of himself he had left behind as he wandered through the house after Antoinette's death, hesitant and wistful as smoke. She curled her hands together and made a church with a steeple, a waggle of people inside. Her thumbs leant together, stubby, determined.

Oh. I don't know exactly. Something unfinished here. Something I've got to do. Something to do with what happened here during the war.

Léonie's shoulders jerked forward. Her profile tautened. The tip of her cigarette winked like a cross red eye.

She said: so you've heard about what happened to Henri's grave. I did wonder. There's going to be an enquiry of course. Lawyers down from Paris. Jewish leaders kicking up a fuss. All those journalists poking around. All the old scandals coming out. Everybody's secrets being dug up.

She puffed on her cigarette. Her mouth pursed round it. Tiny wrinkles there, in the creamy skin, radiating out.

It's no use raking up the past, she said: making people suffer all over again. They want to forget not to remember. I thought we both learned that when we were thirteen years old.

Thérèse relaxed. She felt as though she were made of water. She'd be able to sleep now if Léonie would only go away and leave her alone. She hunted for the words which would send her visitor out.

I'm writing my autobiography. I thought if I wrote down what happened when we were children it would help me to decide what it is I've got to do. But there's so much I've forgotten. You'll have to help me remember.

Léonie curled up tight at the end of the bed, like a caterpillar when you prod it with a twig.

She said: leave my childhood alone. Don't you dare take away anything more of mine.

She added in a calm voice: if you tell any more lies about the past I'll kill you.

She pushed her hair back from her face. Thérèse watched her fingers encounter a hairpin, bring it out, close over it. Wavy-legged, blunt. She herself hadn't needed to use hairpins for years but she remembered the black shininess, the ridges, the thick rounded ends. A hatpin would do better for stabbing. Or one of those special pins they'd used in the convent for securing veils to coifs. Glass-headed. Long and thin. Sharp enough to draw blood.

You always were good at making things up, Léonie said: in your version I was the sinner and you were the saint. Darling little Thérèse, everybody's pet. That's not going to change is it. Yours will be the Authorized Version of what happened won't it.

You've got to be dead before you can be canonized, Thérèse said: and in any case I never pretended I was a saint.

You're a ghoul, Léonie said: picking over what's dead and gone, what's best left undisturbed.

She clambered off the bed, straightened up.

I haven't had to see you for twenty years, she said: for twenty years I could pretend that you *were* dead.

THE PHOTOGRAPHS

When she was little, Léonie was fascinated by the family photographs hung above the bureau in the main *salon*. On to thick grey paper were stuck the pictures that composed Antoinette's view of the present and the past. Red leather gave the collection a definite edge, told where reality started. Glass kept the dust off. If she knelt on the itchy brocade of the little blue armchair, Léonie aged nine could get close to the display, mist it with her breath. She picked her relatives out, one by one.

Antoinette held your eye at the centre. She had chosen to represent herself here with a portrait taken before she became Madame Martin and was just a *mademoiselle*. Her pale hair waved back from her white oval face. She had large blue eyes, a soft round chin. Her hands were clasped in her crepe lap. She'd pasted a polite smile on to her lips, fastened the lace jabot at her throat with a cameo brooch, tucked her feet to one side. High-heeled shoes with a buttoned strap. The buttons – you could just make them out if you screwed up your eyes – were pale knobs, ivory or bone, carved into tightly furled roses. In life, when Antoinette moved, you saw she was a tall woman, long-legged, with broad shoulders and hips. As a girl she'd had red hair, down to her waist Victorine said. Her terrible experiences during the war had sapped her physically, had faded her hair prematurely to pepper and salt. She didn't bother with it after that, just scraped it into a sagging bun at the nape of her neck.

What terrible experiences? Léonie always wanted to know. But Victorine would never say. Or she'd snap: don't be stupid, the war was terrible for everybody. Except the collaborators. And we all know who *they* are.

The photograph of Thérèse showed her in her First Communion

dress, breathless under a net veil and a halo of silk lilies. She clutched her white tulle skirts with gloved hands. A silvery missal was tucked under one arm, a crystal rosary looped over the other. She did not look particularly like her mother. Her curly hair was lighter, almost blonde, and her face was broad, with a pointed chin. She had adjusted herself carefully for the camera. Blue eyes wide and upturned, the hint of a holy smile, white-shod feet turned out in a ballerina position.

Léonie always got her eyes quickly past the photo of herself. Pig-faced, she called it. Green and yellow primary-school uniform of gymslip and blouse. Unruly fair hair cut short, sticking out in frizzy lumps. Blue eyes scowling. Red-cheeked and shiny-nosed; not pretty; and knowing it.

Louis's photograph was stuck next to that of Antoinette in the centre of the fanned collection. He posed stiffly in a tight serge suit, hands on top of his stick, beret on his knee. His mild face was decorated with a brown moustache that drooped over his mouth. An urn and a palm tree sprouted behind him. He sat at the head of the table at meals, and was lord and master in everything, but the house and the farm weren't really his, Victorine had once explained. They were Antoinette and Madeleine's. Louis was only the son of a poor neighbour who managed the farm for the three girls, he'd done very well for himself, marrying in.

Madeleine, two years younger than her sister Antoinette, looked straight out at you, daring you to criticize. She had left home as fast as she could, gone off to study languages in Paris, then married a foreigner she'd met there, gone dancing with when she was supposed to be writing up her notes for class next day. An English journalist. Léonie's father. Clasping Madeleine's arm, he looked like a film star, with a little black moustache and crinkled hair sculpted shiny with brilliantine. Madeleine wore a satin dress with droopy shoulders, a white satin cap perched over one shadowy eye. Her hair was pinned up in rolls and swoops. Her cheekbones stuck out. Her mouth, painted into a cupid's bow, was laughing, eager.

Maurice wasn't in the other, later photographs. He didn't get older and fatter and duller like the other adults did. He stayed fixed as a thin handsome young man with a high forehead and a beaming smile. So full of gaiety, Madeleine always said, remembering: forever cracking jokes. When war broke out he joined up, leaving Madeleine at Blémont with her sister. She chose to stay on, through the years of the Occupation, rather than to go back to the London flat, to give

Antoinette what support she could. I felt I had to, she told Léonie: she needed me. Maurice came home on brief leaves. Léonie was conceived on one of these. She couldn't remember Maurice at all. She told her schoolfriends proudly: my daddy was killed in the war. Madeleine and Léonie were referred to by the others as *les Anglaises*. Madeleine didn't mind, Léonie was sure. Because of Maurice.

Antoinette and Madeleine's older sister had once been called Marie-Joséphine, but she had taken the name of Sœur Dosithée at the Visitation convent in Caen. The deckle-edged photo taken on the day of her profession showed her posed by the crucifix in the centre of the cloister garth. One of her hands stretched out to rest on a pair of bloodied plaster feet with a nail driven through them, thick drops of red paint dripping down. A white cardboardy wimple, thin black veil pinned on top, cut the nun's face to a triangle, black slits in its whiteness for eyes, nose, mouth. The crucifix was of stone carved into roughened tips to make it look like a hewn branch. Behind it marched raw brick cloisters, angular, with few curves.

Sœur Dosithée was the visionary of the family. She had prophesied that Thérèse's birth would be a difficult one. Later, she declared that one of her nieces would become an enclosed contemplative. Don't let it be me, Léonie always prayed.

Victorine was not represented in the group of photographs. She dusted them. She did not count as family, Antoinette explained: because she was their servant.

It was Victorine who took the picture of Thérèse and Léonie that Antoinette declared she disliked yet never got around to removing from the frame. There they stood, merry pair, arms about each other's necks, heads close, grinning at the camera, teetering on the kitchen doorstep. They wore skimpy bunched frocks, little aprons tied on over them. They looked more like sisters than cousins. Antoinette complained that Victorine had got the focus wrong. The children's faces were a smiling blur. You couldn't properly tell which was which.

THE BISCUIT TIN

*T*hérèse became known to Sœur Dosithée only through the letters that Antoinette wrote about her. Frequent letters, throughout the child's infancy and early childhood. Sœur Dosithée, perhaps breaking her vow of poverty, kept all the letters that her sister sent her charting the progress of her little niece. She died when Thérèse was ten.

Antoinette died when Thérèse was only thirteen. Thérèse respectfully sent the nuns a *faire-part*, edged in black; she knew it was the correct thing to do. Shortly afterwards she received a package from the convent in Caen. Her mother's letters, returned to serve as a memento.

Thérèse did not read them immediately. She wrapped them in a piece of pale yellow silk which she tied up with a purple ribbon, and enclosed them in a square biscuit tin which she pushed to the very back of the *buffet*, behind the piles of tablecloths and napkins. The biscuit tin had come from England, part of a Christmas parcel sent by Madeleine. It was printed with coloured pictures of the British royal family, stern in velvet cloaks with fur tops, ugly crowns jammed down over their eyebrows. The paint flaked off over the years. The greaseproof paper lining went yellow. The crumbs and the grains of sugar in the corners shrivelled to nothing. The letters, when Thérèse opened the tin again, smelled of vanilla. She was angry at the time, and she was praying for guidance as to what to do with her life. The letters answered her.

Baby is a little angel, wrote Antoinette to Sœur Dosithée: I do have to admit. I can see already that she is going to be good. Her little eyes look up at me so trustfully, and she sleeps a lot and rarely cries. I'm glad the box of salt cod reached you all safely. I'd like to send you more, but what can one do? These filthy Germans take everything.

But I'm afraid, Antoinette wrote later on to her saintly sister in the convent: I am definitely too frail. I'm too nervous, too weak still, to look after the little one properly, give her all she needs. So Rose Taillé, on the farm here, has taken her. She lost her own baby a week ago, from shock we all think, after her husband was killed, that terrible business I wrote to you about, and she still has plenty of milk. It's a miracle really. It's solved every problem. I'm paying her of course. She keeps Baby with her all the time, so that she can get on with her work while looking after her, it's simpler that way. She carries her in a sling on her back. Lucky child, to be so well cared for while others suffer so much!

Baby loves her rustic life, another letter continued to the black and white sister in Caen: she's grown into a fine healthy creature. I had a peep at her last Sunday. Not letting her see me of course. Just in case. It's better not. My only sorrow is that she's turned out so fair. We've had enough of fair-haired people here to last us a lifetime! Thank God that you've been spared what we've had to go through!

THE IVORY RING

*T*he floor of Rose Taillé's cottage was made of beaten earth covered with lino. Dark blue, with a border of red and yellow squares. A pathway worn across it, between the fireplace, the stone sink, and the door. Lino was lovely stuff in Thérèse's opinion. In the corners of the kitchen, where it fitted badly, it could be prised up, peeled backwards, waggled to and fro until a piece cracked, broke off. Chewed, it eased aching gums: a dirty comforter; flexible chocolate. Then in the cracks between the lino strips lurked crumbs, hairs embedded in solid grease. All to be prodded, tested, gouged out. The world balanced, filthy and delicious, on the tip of her forefinger. She licked it and sucked it in. Such a good baby, Rose confirmed to Madame Martin: happy to play for hours on her own.

In the corner of the dark kitchen sat the child, crooning to herself, eating dried crusts of mud and dung fallen from people's boots as they tramped in and out. Rose found her, snatched her up, tucked her under one arm. Continued to go about opening cupboards, fetching what she needed for making pastry. Being pinioned to a warm soft body: Thérèse liked it. And the firm caress of Rose's arm on her waist. Then she was dumped on one end of the table and given a dab of butter to taste, and, soon, a lump of dough to squeeze, roll into little grey spindles on the floury table-top. She patted it. She smacked it, stabbed it. Laughed, ate it.

She knew Rose's smell, her milk and sweat, her brown skin. She knew the shape of her hips, from riding on them, and the tumbling rhythms of her high-pitched voice. Rose didn't smack her charge: too little; but she would complain at her in exasperated sing-song. Thérèse minded hardly at all; just one note in Rose's music. If the child woke and cried at night, sleepy Rose took her into the warmth of the big bed's flannel sheets, opened her nightdress to her. She'd doze off again with the little one curled like a cat between her stomach and arm.

Bliss. Feeding and being fed. Love was this milky fullness, Thérèse born a second time, into a land of plenty. And she has a good pair of lungs to her, hasn't she, Rose said to her three-year-old son Baptiste: she can scream good and proper that one can. The tearing pains of hunger, her stomach ready to fly apart and explode with raging emptiness, these did not last too long. Need was assuaged. Torture subsided as the searching mouth fastened the breast to it, gobbled, drank. Savage little pig, Rose would shout as the hard gums clamped on to her, then she'd jiggle her, pleased at the child's appetite. This one would not die. This one had been snatched back. And so Rose was patient with her fits of crying and her colic and her teething fretfulness. She walked her up and down the kitchen and sang to her. Thérèse lay over Rose's shoulder, chewing on her ivory ring.

Rose was the world, the sky that curved above you when you first took a tottering step, that held from behind your upstretched hands. She was the spoon that impatiently opened your lips and put artichoke purée between them, the arm that lowered you backwards into the tin bath, the water in which you lay and splashed and did not drown. Thérèse's first word was *Rose*, and by the time she was eighteen months old she could say *cow, apple, duck, cake, dog*. *Maman* was a word she had to be jogged to utter. A blue shape that swam up in the doorway.

Antoinette wore her new blue suit and white beret. Her face was anxious and sweet. A stranger. Thérèse backed away from her. Sharp movements, too pale a skin, the jut of corsets: she rejected them. Louis followed his wife into the kitchen. He'd come straight from the fields, his smell was more what the child was used to. She let him pick her up. Antoinette dropped a bundle of notes on the table for Rose.

Thérèse screamed all the way across the farmyard. She screamed for most of that night until at last she fell asleep. In just a week or so, Antoinette wrote to Sœur Dosithée: she's settled back in very well. She's already forgotten all about Rose, never speaks her name. But how spoilt she's been! She's turned out very clingy. If ever I go out of the room without her she immediately bursts into tears.

THE BABY BOOK

*L*éonie's birthday was a week after Thérèse's, in mid July, just before she and Madeleine set off for their summer holidays with the family in France. Early birthdays were preserved in snapshots: round cakes blazing in the blackness, her own clapped hands in the high chair. She couldn't really remember. When she was ten years old she discovered that she had a past. Madeleine had recorded it in the baby book.

This was shiny and square, with lambs and ribbon knots on the blue cover. Coloured pictures of curly-headed befrocked cherubs with chubby legs dotted its pages. There were headings like Weight When Born, First Stood Alone, First Word.

Aged eighteen months, Léonie read aloud: the little one could say *maman*, baby, *non*, I want, *bonjour*, cat, *maison*.

Madeleine snatched the book away and closed it.

You're not taking that to France. Don't be silly.

I wanted to show it to Thérèse, Léonie said.

She stuffed her toy fox into her duffel bag but allowed his head to peep out. She pulled the string tight, strangling him.

When do we go to France? she asked.

Madeleine threw a bundle of socks at her.

Tomorrow. For the millionth time of telling you.

The sea was Léonie's bed. A long queue of foot passengers waited to get on the overnight boat from Southampton, but the sailors helped the pretty young woman, travelling alone with her daughter, to the front, and up the swaying gangway. Two more followed with her ribbed cloth-covered trunk. Madeleine was so wide-eyed and chic in her full-skirted coat and little hat. The cheery men ran to help. She gave them her best smiles. Then the boat rocked the child. The sea heaved up and down beneath her. Arms, a lap.

The night crossing to France was like a secret. Something sweet whispered in the dark. France loomed unseen. Léonie, inserted between the crisp, tightly tucked-in sheets of her bunk, stayed awake as long as possible. She listened for the siren that marked their departure, the roar of the engines that meant their journey had truly begun. The cabin floor trembled. Madeleine's bottle of scent on the wash-stand jittered. The bunk fell down and up, down and up.

We'll be out of the Solent now, Madeleine said, yawning: into the Channel.

La Manche, it was called in French. To get at French you crossed the sea. The sound of French went up and down like waves rolling in. French was foreign when you were far away, home when you were close. Léonie only half-belonged in it, growing up in England with a dead English hero for a father and a mother disguised as an English missis with English ways. French was what Léonie forgot she could speak. Swore she could not speak. English people in the suburb where she lived despised and hated all foreigners. Wogs and wops they were called. Yids. Léonie was addressed by adults and children alike as Froggy. This term at primary school they'd started learning French. Léonie had discovered that, without ever having been taught a single rule of grammar, she spoke the language perfectly. And now the boat, tiny on the black sea, slipped her across towards it. She was hidden inside. She rode on a great crest of spittle, from one tongue, one watery taste, to another.

For as they left England so they left the English language behind. Familiar words dissolved, into wind and salt spray, ploughed back into foam, the cold dark sea in whose bottomless depths monsters swam, of no known nationality. Halfway across, as the Channel became *La Manche*, language reassembled itself, rose from the waves and became French. While Madeleine snored in the bottom bunk Léonie fought to keep awake, to know the exact moment when, in the very centre of the Channel, precisely equidistant from both shores, the walls of water and of words met, embraced wetly and closely, became each other, composed of each other's sounds. For at that moment true language was restored to her. Independent of separated words, as whole as water, it bore her along as a part of itself, a gold current that connected everything, a secret river running underground, the deep well, the source of life, a flood driving through her, salty breaker on her own beach, streams of words and non-words, voices calling out which were staccato, echoing, which promised bliss. Then the boat churned on. It abandoned English and advanced into French.

In the early morning, standing on deck with her mother, Léonie listened to men in blue jackets shouting to each other in hoarse French. That was how she knew they had arrived. Not because they had reached land, the line of tall thin houses beyond the quay, but because they had docked in French. The secret changeover in the night accomplished and left behind. One normality gone, become foreign. What had been foreign become normal.

There they were, Louis and Antoinette and Thérèse, lined up in a row. Madeleine struggled forward with her bags that the Customs man had marked with a chalk sign, into their cheek-to-cheek embraces. Léonie held on to her toy fox and stared at Thérèse. Her mother's hand on her shoulder reminded her. She gave her cousin an awkward kiss.

Antoinette surveyed her niece.

Léonie is looking quite well, she declared: but her hair has not been properly brushed.

Madeleine linked her arm into Louis's.

New beret? It's very becoming.

He laughed.

Same one you saw last year. And the year before.

Come along, Antoinette said: let's not stand about. The car's over there.

She steered them all with her umbrella, her handbag.

Louis can come back for the trunk tomorrow. Let's get you home and give you something to eat. You look starved, both of you. Don't you have proper food in England?

Léonie climbed into the back of the car after Thérèse. She'd forgotten how she liked its smell: leather, cigarettes, petrol. She thought: now I'm a foreigner again.

THE NIGHT-LIGHT

*I*n the evening, lit by parchment-shaded and gold-pillared lamps, the main *salon* lost its cold angularities and became a place to linger in. As bedtime approached, Léonie tidied herself away into a corner. She squinted at Madeleine's thin ankles, arched foot swinging a high-heeled slipper. Madeleine, now she was in France, had developed a way of sighing, bringing her hands up to clasp the back of her neck, then breathing out explosively. She gave a short, cross laugh, helped herself to another cigarette from the pink and white china box the children were forbidden to touch. Louis reached forward with his lighter then leaned back, smoothing his moustache. Antoinette sat upright, Thérèse perched cross-legged next to her chair. Antoinette's face was energetic and flushed.

Léonie was preoccupied by dread. Perhaps if she admitted she was scared of going out of the room? But Thérèse wasn't, so how could she be? If only she dared ask Madeleine to come too. Her bedroom always felt too big at night. The bed shrank. The skirting-board grew high as her waist. Grotesque bunches of fingers waggled their shadows against the wall near her face, the ceiling peeled back like a tin lid. Her room was on the first floor, at the back, opposite the top of the kitchen stairs. Léonie did not trust a house with two staircases. One carpeted and well-lit, the other narrow and steep, up which something nasty could slink in the darkness to get her. She wished the adults could realize this. But they were busy talking about religion.

But you *must* see that she says her prayers at night, Antoinette exclaimed: how else can you bring her up a good Catholic? If you don't take an interest yourself and give a good example?

Léonie watched the impatient wriggle of her mother's shoulders. In the suburb in London they went to Mass on Sundays but that was that. No point in overdoing it. That was one of Madeleine's maxims. To be applied to everything from religious observance to sweeping the kitchen floor.

Madeleine put down her magazine and her cigarette to kiss the children good night. They passed from her to Louis, who sat at the other end of the sofa reading *Le Figaro*. He stroked their hair and embraced them.

Good night, my little queen, he said to Thérèse: my little flower.

Good night, little thistle, he said to Léonie: my brown pearl.

Antoinette in her stiff-winged armchair sighed over the petticoat she was hemming.

You spoil them, going on like that.

Léonie clung to the handle of the door.

I don't want to go to bed. It's too dark outside.

Be a good girl, Madeleine warned her: run along.

Thérèse took Léonie's hand.

Come on, silly.

Up in five minutes, Antoinette called after them.

There was a low chair at the foot of Léonie's bed. Plump as a *brioche*, with twisted arms and claw legs. Antoinette sat down in it, keeping her back very straight. Everyone had haloes tonight. Downstairs Madeleine's hair flamed in the gold circle of light cast by the lamp. Up here, Antoinette's profile was faintly illumined by the night-light which floated in a saucer of water on the wash-stand by the bed. The stump of candle kept the spiky shadows at a certain distance. They leaped about in the form of imps, black baby devils.

Léonie knelt in front of Antoinette, rested clasped hands on her solid knees. She stretched out the Our Father as long as possible. How completely different it sounded in French. Softer, and grander, both at once. She got through it without a mistake. Antoinette stroked her cheek.

Very good.

Léonie asked: where will I go when I die?

You know what the answer is, Antoinette protested: to heaven, if you're good. Now jump into bed so I can tuck you in.

Léonie kept her hands outside the covers as she had been taught by the nuns at her primary school. The devils trembled towards her as though she wished for them. They opened their mouths to show her sharp tongues and teeth, ready to bite, gobble her up.

She gabbled: I don't like the dark. Dead people come in here and start talking. I don't like them. They start crying.

Antoinette's eyes flew wide open, like a doll's. She stared. Her voice was high and cross.

Really Léonie. You say the most ridiculous things. It's you that talks and starts crying. There are no dead people in this house I assure you. Dead people can't talk. They're in the cemetery, at rest. Don't be so silly.

She blew out the night-light.

Thérèse is asleep already next door. You be a good girl too and go straight to sleep.

The door shut. Antoinette's high heels tapped her away over the wooden floor of the landing, towards the front stairs.

Léonie twisted the corner of her pillowcase into a tight spiral and chewed it. Something ticked in the shadows over by the door. She tried to become flat as the sheet, to stop breathing. She listened. Now it was a shuffle, as of worn loose slippers. A slack tread. Back and forth. Back and forth. And then the voices. That cried out, and chanted, and mourned. In a language she did not want to understand.

THE SILVER CAKE-TRAY

A lane divided the back of the Martin property from the
woods. The lane led to the village one way, and off towards
distant farms the other. So the quickest way to get to the woods, if
you were part of the Martin household, was to enter the orchard
farthest from the house and climb over the vine-clad wall at its end.
You hopped across the clay and stones of the lane, and *voilà*, you
were there.

Victorine went first. She straddled the wall, her basket placed
carefully on the big stone next to her, then hauled the little girls
up and over, one after the other. Their skirts rode up about their
waists, they scratched their legs, their knickers got streaked with
moss. Brambles caught at them as they slithered down.

I'm bleeding, Thérèse shouted: I've got a wound.

Victorine spat on her handkerchief, mopped at the reddened
knee.

Don't make such a noise. If we're very quiet we might just see a
deer. You often do round here.

The three of them stood in the middle of the lane, snuffing up the
keen cold air. Gnarled old apple trees on one side of them, beech trees,
sloping upward, on the other. A curl of green fields on either side. The
entrance to the beech wood was narrow, the end of a funnel. They
waited for some long-legged creature to come stepping delicately out
of the trees. Nothing. So they went in.

It was dark and quiet. No birds in here, calling out, not even the
buzz of a fly, the swish of a cow's tail. Hairy beech husks mashed
under their feet. Smooth brown trunks of the great trees. Sunlight lay
like bits of white rag on the brown floor.

Victorine had no notion of going for walks. She said only the

English, that bizarre race, did that. You went into the fields and woods for what you needed, according to season. Kindling perhaps, or primroses, or mushrooms. Today the hunt was for blackberries, which were known to grow in profusion on the high banks of the fields beyond the woods. From them, mixed with redcurrants and blackcurrants, Victorine produced a notable conserve.

She led the way, singing as she went. A ballad about a soldier returning from war and being wooed by the king's daughter. He beat his drum under her window and she asked him to give her a rose. But he rejected her: too ugly.

Dans mon pays il y a de plus jolies, hummed and frowned Victorine, keeping them in step like the soldier: one two one two.

Suddenly she stopped.

Look. There it is. That's the place.

What? I can't see any.

Not blackberries. The place where the shrine used to be.

An outcrop of white rock from the steep hillside seemed to the children as tall as a cliff. Vivid ferns clung to its foot, where a stream curled across the little clearing. The water came from the base of the rock. It collected there in a stone hollow, fell down over moss. They dipped their fingers in.

What's a shrine? Léonie asked.

Victorine put her hands on her hips. Her small blue eyes were cheerful, contemptuous.

You're so ignorant. You come here every year for the holidays, you live amongst French people, and you still don't know what a shrine is.

She cuffed Léonie lightly on the cheek.

She is, was I mean, a very ancient saint. I don't know her name. Perhaps the Virgin. Her statue used to stand on that ledge of rock, just there above the spring. She had a long pleated dress and bare toes under it, a very young face and long curly hair, and she held a bunch of corn. Or flowers. People brought her gifts. People used to come here all the time, in those days, before the war, to ask for things. Especially for ill children to be cured. They used to leave the children's shoes at the foot of the statue, as a thanksgiving. As a sign.

Thérèse and Léonie stared at the steep wall of rock, at the grass and weeds at its foot. A makeshift altar had been built in front of the spring. A tall heap of boulders, white, somewhat tumbledown.

Then, Victorine went on: when the new priest came, our *curé* that is, he had the shrine destroyed. Rubbish he called it. He said we had to pray in church, not out in the woods. People used to come here at night at harvest festival time and pray and dance. He stopped all that.

Nothing left of the saint that the children could see. Not a stone fingernail. Not a tattered shoe. Nothing except green plants, white rocks, water. Nothing except the altar built in the heart of the wood, next to the spring.

The *curé* was a suave man, dark, with an impassive long face, a thin unsmiling mouth. His words flowed down smoothly as the black cloth of his soutane. Children spotting his tall black shape in the street ran away from him, not towards. Thérèse thought this was because he liked only clever and well-educated people. You had to grow up and get into the *lycée* to have half a chance with him. He was not like the saints you read about who had been parish priests. Not like the *curé* of Ars. Or all the others there must have been. He was more like a cardinal or a bishop, he was so grand. You could see that he would be more than a match for some small female saint with no name.

Did he smash up the statue himself? Léonie asked: or did he put her away somewhere?

I don't know, Victorine said: it was all pulled down from one day to the next, and you know it happened during the war, everything was topsy-turvy then. The statue just vanished.

She spat on the ground.

The Germans did their fair share of tearing up the woods. Using them for their filthy business.

What filthy business? Thérèse asked.

Killing people of course, Victorine said.

She pointed at the spring.

This was once a powerful place. Full of magic. Not any more.

They trooped through the sunlit darkness, keeping close together, and came out halfway up the hill on to the slope where the blackberries grew.

Do you still hate the Germans? Léonie asked.

Of course, Victorine said: when you think of what they did to people here. To Rose Taillé for example.

What did they do? asked Thérèse.

Oh, Victorine said: you're too young to understand. One day when you're older I'll tell you.

She was red in the face. She twiddled a strand of her frizzy blonde hair. She screwed up her mouth and regarded them.

Let's get on and pick blackberries.

THE CARPETS

The war was a sort of bookmark which divided the pages of history. Victorine mentioned it casually all the time. Before the war we. After the war he. During the war they.

The local children just ran wild all over the place, Victorine said: I remember them riding the cows and holding cow races, oh those children had a lovely war.

Better than now, then, Thérèse said: not having to help with housework I bet.

They were dusting the main *salon*. Thérèse and Léonie did the unbreakable things, like the legs of chairs, the tops of tables, the strip of tiled floor showing between the carpet and the wall.

You can't imagine what it was like, Victorine stated: Germans everywhere. They billeted the men all over the village and even in our outbuildings here. And the officers took over the house.

She began to inspect the children's handiwork.

Haven't you ever wondered, she said to Thérèse: why your mother had these carpets put down?

Thérèse threw her duster in the air and caught it.

I couldn't care less. Can't we go and play outside now? We're finished in here.

Victorine stooped and lifted a corner of the carpet.

Look. See? The marks of the Germans' boots. All over the ground floor it used to be beautiful red tiles, spotless. Now it's all ruined, every inch.

Léonie peered at the pockmarks in the red surface. The memory of the house made visible. Scars that would never fade. The injuries of the house lived on, under the carpet which concealed them. Once you knew they were there, you could not forget.

One of the girls from the village, Victorine went on: used to come out to help me with the cleaning. In the end she took to sleeping here, it was easier. We gave her one of the little rooms upstairs, at the back.

Her glance crossed Léonie's. Her voice became casual.

Well, she got very friendly with one of the German officers billeted here. I used to see her creeping up to his room at night. Of course *he* had one of the big ones at the front.

Why? Thérèse asked: what for?

Victorine stared at her reflection held in the ornate frame of the mirror over the fireplace while her fingers dusted the china vases that flanked it.

Anyway, nowadays she runs one of the bakeries here, that one we never go into. That's why we don't go there. Didn't you know? She's very respectable nowadays. Oh yes. But we never visit her shop and she knows why. We'd rather starve than go in there.

Oh, Thérèse said: you mean a *collaborator*.

She lifted her chin.

Vive la France! Vive de Gaulle!

THE RECIPE BOOK

Victorine was juggling with potatoes, to make the little girls laugh. She could keep three in the air at once, a skill she said she taught herself after she was taken once, as a child, to the circus.

Gougère for supper, she sang out: Thérèse, find the recipe for me.

The recipe book lay on the table. Stiff blue cardboard covers, battered and cracked, pages of coarse paper yellow at the edges. Printed in wartime. The book's old-fashioned typeface, cramped and black, was as distinctive as Victorine herself in her dark dress and blue check overall, rapt lady clown with a glistening face and deft wrists.

She came, panting, to a halt. They applauded. She tossed the potatoes, hop hop hop, into the basket held by Léonie, then bowed. She tied a big red-and-white-striped drying-up cloth around each of their waists and made them kneel up to the table on chairs.

Peel the *patates* for me for the soup, she said: and I'll keep the pan of *choux* mixture for you to lick. I'll make a cake too.

French cakes, Léonie mused: aren't as good when they come out of the oven as English cakes. No currants and raisins. No icing. No hundreds and thousands or anything.

French cooking, Victorine asserted: is the best in the world!

Her blue eyes narrowed to marble chips. She pushed back a long fair curl with one hand. She whacked butter and eggs with her wooden spoon.

Suet pudding with slabs of butter and white sugar, Léonie recited: fried eggs and bacon, fish and chips, kippers, marmalade, proper tea, Eccles cakes.

Thérèse flicked a piece of muddy potato peel across the table.

Everyone knows that English food is terrible, she stated: soggy boiled vegetables in white sauce, overcooked meat, I don't know how your mother could stand it, having to go and eat stuff like that. She stopped being really French, everyone says so. The English are just heathens, aren't they Victorine?

Heathens was a word Victorine applied to foreigners. Who were not Catholics. The people in the famous circus, for example, that she was always telling them about.

Léonie frowned very hard so that she would not cry. She concentrated on her potato, gouging out its deep black eye with the serrated tip of her knife. The potato was called Thérèse.

Tell us about the circus, Thérèse said to Victorine: tell us about the costumes that shone in the dark.

Thérèse loved hearing about the padded silver suit of the terrifying and sad white clown. The pale blue tights, moulded over bulging thighs, of the male trapeze artists, that made you think about the flattened bulge between their legs. The frayed leopard skin, that left one muscled shoulder bare, of the strong-man lion tamer. Victorine perched in the darkness on a wooden bench with no back, feet dangling over the steep invisible ground. Smell of sweat and hot straw and animals. Then the toot of a trumpet and the clown with the enormous sorrowful eyes was coming at her in her ring-side seat and she wanted to run away.

The circus, Victorine began, pushing the bowl of cake mixture towards them: was run by gypsies.

She dropped her voice to a scratchy whisper.

It used to be said that the gypsies stole little children. Little curly-haired blonde children. And then killed them.

Thérèse sucked her fingers.

What!?

Yes. Just like the Jews. People used to say that the Jews liked to steal Christian children and babies. They killed them and then used their blood for baking the Passover bread.

Really?

Of course no one believes that any more. But people used to.

Thérèse said: the Church says we have to pray for the Jews to be converted to the one true faith.

Léonie was confused: Jesus was a Jew wasn't he?

Yes, silly, but then he invented Christianity, didn't he, so all the Jews were supposed to stop being Jews and be Catholics instead. Only they wouldn't. They had Jesus put to death. It was their fault, really, that Jesus was on the cross. They were as bad as the communists. You have to pray for them, that they'll repent.

Oh.

Léonie went on licking the cake mixture out of the bowl. Her Catholic primary school in the north London suburb had many Jewish pupils. When she went home to tea with them she ate delicious food. Bagels with cream cheese and smoked salmon, pumpernickel bread, gherkins, rollmops, chollah bread, pastries rich with poppyseed and cinnamon. But now she denied that memory. She ran her forefinger around the inside of the white pyrex bowl and said nothing.

A little later on she went to find her mother. Madeleine was sitting at the red and black wicker table in the little conservatory at the back of the house, pinning a paper pattern on to the green and blue paisley material she had spread out in front of her. She looked surprised to see Léonie.

Whatever are you doing indoors on such a lovely afternoon? You should be off out playing with Thérèse.

We were helping Victorine, Léonie said: anyway it's nearly supper-time.

Madeleine frowned.

You shouldn't spend so much time with her you know. You should do things on your own with Thérèse more. She's your hostess after all.

Léonie stroked the pattern with her fingertip, to flatten it. She took a silver pin and inserted it where a dart was marked with a black V and a dot. Madeleine picked up a pair of pinking shears and began to slice through the material.

Did Daddy like coming here? Léonie asked: did he like this house?

Madeleine was now absorbed in her task. She bent over the pattern, her strong fingers guiding her scissors. Her voice was no longer the fussy one she put on for ticking Léonie off. It was warmer, more amused.

Oh he loved it. He got on really well with Louis you know. They were friends, even before Louis married Antoinette. They used to sit here together for hours, smoking their pipes and chatting. They'd take their *apéritifs* in here before lunch, and their coffee afterwards.

Or Maurice would go out and help Louis on the farm. He loved Antoinette too. He understood how she needed me when war broke out and most of the men were away, he realized I wouldn't feel able to go back to England and abandon her. He said: don't worry, old girl, you've got two homes now, that's all.

The cut-out sleeve flopped neatly on to one side of the table. It had a paper lining, like a thin white shadow, fine and smooth to the touch. The paisley cloth hid underneath.

Haven't I ever told you the story about Maurice helping Louis hide all the wine? Madeleine said: that'll show you how much your father liked this place.

She spread out another section of paisley cloth and pinned another bit of pattern on to it. The second sleeve.

There's not much to tell really. It was when Paris fell and the Germans were occupying everywhere. People in the village could imagine what it would be like, the Germans taking all their supplies. So they got together and decided to hide their cider and wine so the Germans shouldn't have it. Our cellars are so big, they put it there, under a great heap of sand. Louis and Maurice and Henri Taillé worked all night, digging. Hundreds of bottles they buried. The Germans never found them. Well, once they nearly did. When Antoinette, when she . . . Well. But it was all right in the end. After the war everybody got their wine and cider back. They knew Maurice had helped. They were grateful to him. They knew he loved France.

No quiver in Madeleine's voice. She snipped serenely. Her scissors took long delicate strides. The cloth fell apart as they advanced. Léonie left her to it and returned to the kitchen.

It was empty. It smelled of hot cake rising in the oven. She put her hand on the wooden knob of the kitchen table drawer. A popping wooden eye level with her chest. Like Pinocchio's nose it could shoot in and out. In here Victorine kept old butter papers, pieces of string, loose boiled sweets, old corks, red-stained, with their sweetish smell of wine. Also in here she kept the key to the cellar door. Léonie scrabbled at the back of the drawer and drew it out.

THE CELLAR KEY

*T*he cellar door was in one corner of the kitchen, near the window on the outside wall. Its paint glistened black. It was kept locked, and entry to it forbidden to the children, as Léonie knew perfectly well. Another door led into the cellar from outside in the yard, and that too was kept locked.

The cellar, being a sort of tunnel between yard and house, would have made an excellent place to play in on wet days. Too dark, too dangerous, said Antoinette: easy to cut yourself on a broken wine bottle or get your frock filthy with cobwebs and dust. Léonie had never been bothered by the prohibition; there were so many other intriguing sites for play. Now she thought: how mean grown-ups are. I'm going to see what it's like in there.

The black iron key turned easily in the lock. The door swung open inwards. A china light-switch, finger-flicked, showed her a narrow wooden staircase. She hesitated, then crept down.

The stone coolness below the house smelled of soil. She stood on a floor of trodden earth. The single light-bulb dangling on its long black cord showed her rows of iron racks. The heels of wine bottles were cold green moons she stroked as she slid past. A tall barrel had split its sides, gaped. She stopped when something soft and fluttery brushed her face. She was deeper than the house, level with worms, all the dead things that were put into the ground. Had that been a spider's web that touched her cheek just now? Where was the heap of sand? Perhaps it was time to go back upstairs.

The light went out. The door into the kitchen slammed. Léonie stood on the bottom step and clutched the metal handrail. Black water lapped her, depths she could not see into. When she opened her mouth to shout, darkness filled it, a black biscuit tasting of wine.

She was part of the shadows now. Not Léonie any more. She was dissolving, into musty air.

The door above flew open. Oblong blaze of light from the kitchen. Antoinette's legs, white and bare, black and white folds of her dress skimming her knees, her sandalled feet bound in black straps.

Her voice was shrill.

The cellar light's gone. There's someone down there. Who is it? What are you doing? Victorine! Madeleine! Come here!

Léonie turned her face upwards.

It's me, Aunt.

You gave me such a shock, Antoinette cried out: come out of there this minute do you hear?

Now that she had to leave it, the cellar was suddenly a friendly place. In the kitchen she shrank before her aunt's wrath and trembling hands.

You know it's the one thing I really can't stand, Antoinette shouted: disobedience.

Madeleine spoke from the doorway. A warning, from one grown-up to another.

Don't let yourself get into a state. She didn't realize. She doesn't know about the cellar. I told her the story about the wine, that's all. She just wanted to have a look.

Antoinette locked the cellar door and flung the key on the table.

Why don't you all just leave me alone.

THE RED SUITCASE

*A*ntoinette's suitcase was bound in scarlet cloth. She was weighed down by it. She dragged it across the Customs Hall. She had got off the boat and was looking for the way out. Léonie followed her. None of the uniformed Customs men would touch the red suitcase, let alone chalk a squiggle on the side and allow it through. Back and forth Antoinette went, ever more urgently. Léonie crept behind. Red and dangerous, that suitcase. The Customs men knew it. They'd been tipped off. A bomb inside it, timed to explode and tear them all to shreds. Red shreds of flesh. Antoinette began to run. Watched by Nazi soldiers through plate-glass doors.

Léonie's bed was stinking and wet. She sat up, crying. Already she could hear the scolding she was sure she'd get. Ten years old and you've wet the bed! Really, at your age, this is too much. She was too frightened to get out of bed and go to find Victorine. The room was full of her aunt's mad red grin.

THE SOFA

The doctor's car was long and black. It crunched round on the gravel in front of the house then sped off through the gates scattering white stones. Madeleine shut the gates. She came back slowly towards the house. Seeing Thérèse and Léonie watching her from an upstairs window she straightened up, smiled, waved.

Come on, Victorine bullied: no nonsense, put that frock on and don't argue please, Thérèse.

She screwed a wetted face flannel into a point and dug it into Léonie's ears, then attacked her unruly hair with a hard brush. The dresses, in cotton voile, were scratchy with starch. The children took deep breaths, tried to shrink their shoulder-blades, as the buttons were done up at the back. The puff sleeves were too tight under the armpits, pinched your flesh. Crocheted white socks, crunch at heel and toe, black patent strap shoes crammed on over them, and Léonie and Thérèse were ready. They leered at each other, then tittupped down the polished wood of the stairs, clutching the banisters. Soles slippery, wanting to skate.

Mind you behave, Victorine called after them: don't give us cause to be ashamed of you.

The ladies of the village had already arrived, and were sitting with Antoinette in the white *salon*. This was a ground-floor room which bulged out on the side of the house looking towards the big lawn and the stables. Having windows in three of its walls, it was always full of light. A severe light. A chaste light. The room was as coldly white as death. White brocade wallpaper, white muslin at the windows, white porcelain statues on the mantelpiece and the occasional tables, white lace of the shawl folded across the arm of the sofa.

Antoinette reclined here, surrounded by the doctor's wife, the pharmacist's wife, the teacher's wife. All in silk frocks, gloves, hats. The hairs on the back of Thérèse's neck rose up and shouted Danger. Sombre colours. Hushed voices. Troop of old crows, she thought: coming to peck us about. Hand in hand with Léonie, she advanced, as yet unseen.

The sofa was upholstered in yellow and blue satin, shiny and tight, finished with rolled gold cord and tassels. A hard little matching satin bolster tucked in at either end. Gold claws at the end of twisted wooden legs. Antoinette did not seem comfortable. She looked as though she might slide off at any moment. The sofa merely tolerated her. Any moment it would buck, toss her, white broken heap, on to the gleaming floor.

The ladies looked up. Thérèse bounded forward, toe pointed, all smiles, ruffles, to receive pats, petting, kisses. She leaned against her mother's shoulder, stroked her hair, cheek to cheek. Léonie, sweaty-palmed, shook hands all round. Antoinette smiled, pointed.

The little girls retreated to the padded bench in the bay window. They stretched their ears across the room to hear the tut-tuts, mutterings, to decode the sighs and silences which surrounded them.

When.

If God wills.

A long remission, he thought?

Then.

So.

The white *salon* was thick with feeling. Sturdy as the white blancmange that Léonie hated and thought she had left behind in England. Now here it was in France, glutinous, gloating.

Why ever didn't you send for him before?

Working too hard for years.

Victorine came in with the tray of tea. *Tartines* of yellow sweet bread soaked pink with blackcurrant jam for the children, a slice each of set custard with a blackened skin, wrinkled and curdy. Flavoured with nutmeg. Léonie felt sick. She tugged at Thérèse's skirt. Antoinette noted this gesture, clapped her hands.

Go on children, run outside and play.

They loitered at the front of the house, at the garden corner, sharp angle of white stone, and scowled at one another. Strangers because of their clean clothes they must not tear or get dirty. Léonie the lumpish foreigner forgetting her French, hot and red-faced, scuffing the point of her shoe on the gravel. Everything she hated was white: that slice of custard just now; these little stones hard as sugared almonds at a christening; the cones of rice, curly as white hyacinths, floating in a sea of whipped egg white, that they had as a supper treat; the damask of the tablecloth that her sweaty palms would soil; the chilly marble of the fireplace in the white *salon*; the glistening pearls of tapioca that lurked at the bottom of soup. Breast cancer, she thought, was white. Whiteness of skin and bones, bandages, hospitals. All the words adults did not say.

But Thérèse liked white. She liked the words that described it: spotless, pure, immaculate. She approved of the crispness of the linen coifs of nuns, the ironed cleanness of her mother's Sunday gloves, the drift of long tulle skirts that had stirred about her on her First Communion day, the soft transparency of the veils of village brides. She was delighted when Louis called her his little snowflake, his little flower, little lily of the valley. She imagined the doctor wrapping her sick mother in white quilts, white fleeces, white blankets.

Léonie shut her eyes and frowned. She did like some white things. Yes. The sugar icing on cheap currant buns at home in England, a thick layer, that cracked then melted. She opened her eyes again, winked at Thérèse.

Let's go and play in the cellar. Victorine won't know, she's still busy dishing out the tea.

Thérèse hesitated. On a day so out of the ordinary, wearing her best summer frock, she was perhaps entitled to behave in an unusual way? She decided she would be disobedient. She crept after Léonie. They glided down the wooden stairs.

Dirty cobwebs dangled from the brick vaults arching above their heads. The wine racks were dusty. Thérèse drew her forefinger across the cool iron and traced a zigzag. Then she leaned forward and blew the dust away. She stood up very straight, stretched her arms out in front of her, shut her eyes.

Look. I'm being a sleepwalker. Like you when you were little.

The pool of light in which they stood was sharply divided from the darkness pressing up around like a stealthy animal. Léonie shivered.

More like a ghost, she whispered.

Thérèse felt her way around a barrel as tall as she was. She vanished. Léonie counted the seconds. Waiting for the thunder. This was the sound of Thérèse tripping and falling over. Léonie thrust herself into the musty blackness behind the barrel, found an arm, two arms, pulled. They tumbled back together into the lit space at the bottom of the stairs, gasping.

Look what I found, Thérèse said: right at the back by the wall. You'll never guess.

A ladylike shoe in worn red velvet, with a wonky high heel and an ankle-strap fastened with a bone button carved into the semblance of a rose.

It is isn't it? Thérèse said: one of the pair Maman's wearing in the photograph. The shoes she had when she was a young girl.

She brushed dust off the toe.

She never said she lost it.

Léonie was bored.

Well why should she? I expect she had plenty of others.

Not in the war you dolt, Thérèse said: they had to make shoes out of wood and cork, Victorine said so.

Léonie looked at her cousin with satisfaction. The bow trailed in her untidy hair, her face and arms were smudged with dust, the skirt of her dress was torn.

Thérèse had had enough. She turned towards the stairs.

We'll be in such trouble. You shouldn't have made me come down here.

But nobody bothered them when they returned to the white *salon*. The ladies had gone, and Madeleine and Louis were sitting with Antoinette in silence. They didn't seem to notice the children's dishevelment. They were very still. Staring at the empty air.

Thérèse put on a joyous smile, skipped up to the sofa to kiss her mother. Antoinette looked at the object clutched in her daughter's hand. Patches of red appeared on her cheeks like bits of worn red velvet. She seized the shoe and threw it into the fireplace.

Really. At your age you should know better than to bring rubbish into the house.

THE SACK

The children haven't noticed anything, Madeleine said: they're too young. All they think about is playing.

She was talking to Victorine in the kitchen. Léonie and Thérèse were down the other end, putting on their boots. They were getting ready to go out with Louis.

The bull had got loose from his tether. The current in the electric fence surrounding that particular field had been turned off, since the bull was made fast to a stake by a thick rope. Somehow he had worked himself free. At any moment he might trample into the road, lower his head, run at someone. Louis and the two girls set out to catch and resecure him.

He was grazing near the edge of the field, where the grass was juicy and thick. Thérèse and Léonie lay flat on their stomachs, heads well down, just where the long grass began, peeping through the stems itchy with insects. They longed to sneeze but did not dare. Very close reared the great bull. They could hear the rasp of his breath as he tossed his head against the cloud of flies that haloed it.

The soles of Louis's boots wriggled forwards. His behind, in rubbed brown corduroy, heaved and sank. His bony wrist snaked out, towards the trailing end of the bull's rope. His voice hissed back to them.

Got him!

They ran into the kitchen, shouting to Victorine.

We've been in danger. Could have been gored.

Victorine looked over their heads at Louis.

Madame's back from seeing the specialist. Doesn't sound too good, she says.

I know, Thérèse shouted: let's go and look at the kittens.

The cat had made a sort of nest in one corner of the stables. In its depths struggled small blind creatures, curled, feeble. Léonie and Thérèse knelt down in the straw. The squeak of the stable door made them turn round.

Baptiste Taillé had followed them in. He was a stocky boy of middle height, with blue eyes, a bristling crew cut, and red cheeks. His trousers, made of what looked like sacking, were chopped off at the knee, held up by a strap wound round his middle. He wore a thick jumper, and wellingtons.

He picked up a kitten by its tail and swung it to and fro in the air, laughing at its cries.

They're all going to be drowned today, he sang: are you going to come and watch?

He began to toss the kitten from hand to hand. Léonie and Thérèse pretended not to notice him. It was a way of preserving social divisions. A certain distance had to be kept. Baptiste broke the rules. He picked up a second kitten, dangled one from each hand, swung them so that they hit each other. He whistled. His bright eyes dared the girls to challenge him.

They turned their backs. Léonie caught herself feeling sorry that this had to be so. That silent disapproval had to emanate from her and Thérèse in order to prove that they were young ladies, to provoke him to further displays of cruelty. A stupid game dedicated to shoring up the notion that they did not want to play together. She gave the mother cat a final pat, sighed, put her nose in the air, and followed Thérèse out of the stable.

Eengleesh peeg, Baptiste shouted after them.

They clambered up the rickety wooden outside staircase to Louis's workshop in what had been the grooms' quarters. Here he mended chairs, weaving fresh straw into the seats, fixing wobbly legs. He regilded picture frames, glued back together broken cups and plates. Today he sat surrounded by paints and solvents, balls of string, boxes of old cotton reels and electrical parts, but he wasn't working. He was twiddling a piece of cork and sucking on his empty pipe.

The children stood on the top step and spoke to him over the half-door.

Is it true the kittens have got to be killed?

Drowned, Louis said: yes. This afternoon.

He remembered who they were. He stretched his face into a smile, lifted his hand.

Be off, little queen. I'm busy just now.

After lunch the girls hid behind the kitchen door and peered round it. Louis came from the stables with a blanket-wrapped bundle in his arms.

Chloroform, whispered Thérèse: so that they won't feel anything.

Louis upended the bundle into the rainwater-butt. That was all. The dead creatures, fished out, their fur sleek with wet, were smaller than rats. Baptiste appeared with a sack into which he scooped the corpses. Man and boy went off together in the direction of the kitchen garden.

Léonie shouted: I'm starving. How long until tea-time?

Thérèse whispered: Rose Taillé only has one eye but he's got two. He's quite normal considering.

Only one eye? Léonie asked.

She fell on a pitchfork when she was little, Thérèse said: everyone knows that. First she was blind and then when she was a bit older they fitted her with a glass eye. You can tell which one it is, it's green. Her other one's blue.

His are blue, Léonie said.

To herself she thought: I want to look at him again to see exactly what colour.

She bit delicately into her slice of bread and jam.

Of course they are, Thérèse said: everyone round here's got blue eyes. Even you, half-English.

Half-French, Léonie didn't bother reminding her. She concentrated on the face in her mind's eye, the single eye that saw in the dark and coloured things in.

THE ALTAR

When she married Louis, Antoinette changed the house a bit, to modernize it. She had two bathrooms put in, and she had a dressing-room built, next to her bedroom. This was a sort of passage, short, lined with cupboards. A long swivel mirror collected the light in one corner. A white sink shone at the far end, some sort of covered porcelain bucket underneath it. A green rug tousled in front of the door. Stockings and petticoats, discarded for the wash, lounged about in here, flung over the back of a carved armchair. Pink silk trimmed with tea-coloured lace, damp nylon. Smell of soap, cedarwood, camphor.

It was an un-dressing room, Thérèse thought. The place where her mother, clad in an old kimono, slumped on the low chair and held whispered conversations with Victorine. Worse even than the ladies in the white *salon*. They lowered their voices right down to the floor. They hissed, as evil as geese. Their wings flared and beat the air. Hanging about on the other side of the open door, you wanted to screech then run.

Thérèse persuaded her mother to let her change bedrooms, to take one on the floor above. She put her request prettily, asking for peace and quiet to study in, more space for books and plants. Away from certain words, from the atmosphere of dressing-rooms, was what she meant. Antoinette, anxious that her illness should not upset her daughter in any way, agreed immediately.

Thérèse spent a day rearranging her things, then invited her cousin up to take a look.

It's a bit like a chapel isn't it, Léonie said.

On the far wall, opposite the door, was a big black wooden crucifix. Underneath it, a little table bore blue candles, statues of Our Lady and the saints, and miniature vases of daisies, all arranged on a bit of old sheet with a cross painted on the front.

Léonie asked: but where's your doll? Don't you play with her any more?

Thérèse pointed. There was a shoebox at the foot of the makeshift altar. Léonie went over to have a look.

She's dead, Thérèse said: that's her there, in her coffin.

Léonie took the lid off. She folded back the quilt of cottonwool scattered with gold paper stars. The baby doll's blue glass eyes winked at her. It was naked. Its gold nylon curls had been yanked out. It was quite bald.

She's not dead, Léonie protested: not yet. Not if we operate. We might be able to save her.

She pursed her lips and looked at Thérèse.

I'd better practise on you first. Just to make sure I do it right.

In the end they took turns to be the surgeon. The patient lay on the bed to be got ready. Her body was swathed in towels, except for the gap where her vest was pulled up. The surgeon prodded the shivery flesh, searching for the tumour that must be removed. The comb-scalpel parted the patient's chest in two. It tickled, and the patient had to be shushed. The bath-sponge tumour was lifted out and dropped into the soap-dish by the bed. Then a fountain-pen needle stitched up the lips of the wound in a neat blue herringbone pattern.

Second time around they added refinements. An anaesthetic was administered by injection. The sleeping patient's eyes were bandaged, just in case she tried to anticipate what the surgeon would do next. She was gagged, and tied to the bed with the cord of Thérèse's dressing-gown. The surgeon took off her own clothes as well as the patient's.

Victorine's voice issued up from the garden below the windows, demanding to know where they were. They padded down the backstairs. The kitchen was empty. Léonie raised the heavy round lid of the range and Thérèse slid the expired doll in her shoebox into the hissing tumble of red. They waited for the space of one Hail Mary, then ran out into the yard to call for Victorine.

THE DARK GLASSES

*T*he news of Sœur Dosithée's holy and resigned death came on a black-edged card in a black-edged envelope. Joy had surrounded her final hours. Now, after her long fight against cancer, she rested in the arms of Jesus for evermore.

Louis frowned while he read this out to Madeleine and the children at lunch. He put the card down and began serving out the *œufs soubise* from the dish in front of him.

Antoinette's too ill to go to the funeral, he said: and mustn't be left. And I've far too much to do on the farm. So that's that.

Madeleine picked up her fork and began to eat. This was the sign that the children could start eating too. Léonie tucked in. *Oeufs soubise* was one of her favourite dishes. Creamy onion sauce slathered over lightly boiled eggs. She'd never caught the French trick of eating slowly, relishing the food. She gobbled. She was, she told herself in excuse, so extremely hungry.

Thérèse wasn't. She looked at her father over the top of her full plate.

Darling Papa, couldn't we go to the funeral together? You and me? She was my godmother after all.

Louis lifted his shoulders.

You're too young, little one. Little girls of ten shouldn't be thinking about dreary things like funerals.

Thérèse went and stood next to him. She rubbed her face against his sleeve. Often this made him laugh and hug her. Today he shook her off. He spoke to Madeleine.

That dreary Godforsaken convent. I went there for the clothing, because Antoinette wanted me to take photographs. But never again, God help me. I was always against her burying herself there.

Léonie swished her fork around her plate to gather up the last vestiges of *sauce mornay*.

Tante Antoinette wanted to be a nun too, didn't she? she remarked: when she was young. Before the war. She told me so. Ages ago.

Louis snapped: don't talk with your mouth full.

To console Thérèse for missing the funeral, that afternoon they played a new game. Carmelites.

We'll call it, Thérèse said: all for love.

Carmelites were brown like caramels. Carmelite hermits did not eat sweets but fasted, in their desert huts, on delicacies like fried locusts, grasshoppers, and crushed beetles. They slept on piles of old sacks in the disused pigsty, had long beards and staffs, and went barefoot. Since it was very hot they just put on a loincloth, but when they had visitors they might throw on a leopard skin to look more venerable. When wicked women called Charlottes came to tempt them the hermits cast off all their clothes and rolled naked in the patch of nettles behind the pigsty. Thérèse objected to realism at this point. She said pretending would do just as well.

Léonie played the Charlotte. She copied her costume from a film poster in the *bar-tabac* in the village. She wore her swimsuit, with a plastic mac, left open, on top of it, dark glasses, several strings of plastic popper beads, and a pair of fluffy pink mules abandoned by Victorine to their dressing-up box. She wound a lime chiffon scarf of Madeleine's around her head, and practised pouting with one hip thrust forward.

Her role was to distract the holy Thérèse, who sat reading the local newspaper inside the pigsty, and make her look up. She purred and flirted to no avail.

Very good, Thérèse conceded afterwards: just like the Devil would do.

The Devil's handmaid can never win in this game, Léonie pointed out: it's not fair.

Thérèse threw down her newspaper.

All right then. Let's play martyrs.

They sat on the floor of the pigsty catacomb, praying. They wept and clanked their chains and speculated on how it would feel to be eaten alive by the lions.

I'll be the lion, Léonie said: bags I the lion.

First she posed as a Roman centurion and did a bit of torture. It was a way of working herself up to full ferocity. She stretched Thérèse on the rack until her bones cracked, tore off her breasts with red-hot pincers, then flogged her with twigs and broke her on the wheel. Thérèse refused to stop being a Christian. Her punishment for this was to be thrown into the arena. To be torn apart by wild animals.

The first time they tried out death in the arena the Christian got infected by the general bloodlust and bit the lion. Léonie rubbed her arm, very cross.

You've got to die without making any fuss. That's the whole point.

They began again. Léonie, on all fours, shuffled towards the saint and growled. Her teeth gripped Thérèse's leg. None too gently. Thérèse rolled her eyes upwards to heaven, smiled heroically, and fell over. Léonie pawed the dust.

Too soon!

They tried once more. Now Léonie's mane stuck out crisply, the blaze of a sunflower, and her fur was yellow as bananas. She scratched herself, searching for fleas. She snarled as she leapt from her subterranean tunnel out into the sunlight, on to the bloodstained sand. She swished her thick tail. She strolled.

Thérèse lurked in the corner, kneeling, hands clasped. The lion got near enough to blow hot oniony breath into her face. The lion smiled and opened her jaws.

The martyr shrieked: I'm doing a miracle, you can't stop me.

She unfurled a palm. On it lay the silky brown square of a caramel. The lion roared. Her tongue slunk out. A rasping lick on the martyr's hand and the caramel was gone.

The lion purred. Did her trick to catch the saint who avoided becoming a martyr. Lay down on her back, rolled over, waved her paws. The saint could not resist the appeal of that spotted belly, butter-soft, that pale fur so *douce* and plush. She leaned forwards and stroked the lion. Contented, planning her sermon. Virgins made invincible by God, something like that. With a silver breastplate stuck full of arrows and the roars of the bloodthirsty pagans turned to weeping and conversion.

The lion jumped up, pounced. She batted the saint smartly on to the floor, pinned down her flailing arms and legs with her own.

I've won I've won, Léonie crowed: I've beaten you.

You haven't, Thérèse screamed: I'm better than you, I'll show you, I'll never speak to you again.

They rolled in the dust, fighting, until they were exhausted and filthy. Then side by side they lay still, heads pillowed on the pile of dressing-up clothes, bodies slack. They were sweaty, and hot. They let the warm air roll over them like water. For a long time they did not speak. Their fingers slid inside each other's clothes, over each other's skin, stroking, testing. Then further, into the little purses that must never be talked about, that they weren't supposed to know they had. They were breathless, they jumped, they shut their eyes tight.

Thérèse called it dying. The moment in the game when the martyr's soul began its slow slip away to heaven. But it was too sweet, Léonie thought: how could it be called dying, most intensively living more like.

This is what heaven's like, Thérèse said: it's like this for Aunt Dosithée all the time.

And Léonie wondered: in heaven can you have the lion also, and the soft belly, and the fight?

THE SOAP-DISH

*T*he lavatory at the far end of the yard, Victorine told the
puzzled children: was the only one in the house when it was
first built.

Why? Léonie asked.

I don't know, Victorine said, rolling out her pastry: but people used
pots in those days didn't they. It wasn't only children who used pots,
everyone did.

The little shed still smelled of those days when it had been used.
Léonie loved sniffing about it. A rich and powerful odour, not
unpleasant outside here in the yard where the air was already
scented with manure and compost, with the melons ripening in
the wire *garde-manger*, with whatever was rotting in the dustbins.
A man used regularly to come and take the shit away, Victorine had
explained. Well, it would go on the fields, wouldn't it? Louis, catching
Léonie lifting up the mahogany flap in the seat of what looked like
one of the pews in church, forbade her future entry. Then he nailed
up the shed door.

Honestly Léonie, Thérèse said: you are disgusting.

She linked her arm in Louis's, and looked up at him through her
eyelashes. He stroked her cheek.

Léonie did not want to watch Thérèse clamber on his knee, twist
her blonde curls with one finger, ogle him. She retreated to the
kitchen. She watched Victorine glance out of the window, seize a
shovel and bucket, dash outside.

Baptiste Taillé had given her the signal. He winked at Léonie who
pottered after her.

Two carthorses gone past, he announced: lots of good shit.

All three hurried round the side of the house and issued through the gates on to the road. Loose orange heaps, recently dropped, steaming, that bristled with straw. Very good for the vegetable garden, Léonie knew. She watched Victorine and Baptiste scoop it up. Half for the Martins, half for Baptiste's mother Rose.

Children's shit was of no use to anyone. Was dropped into a disinfected gaping hole, discreetly, behind a locked door. Must never be talked about. Only adults could do that, when they checked on your health. Léonie never needed any help to go. No suppositories for her, no thank you. If she could tell no one else she admitted to herself that she did like shit. Her own. The act.

Louis always occupied the lavatory straight after breakfast. He disappeared with his copy of *Le Figaro* and his pipe. He was not to be rushed. He was gone a fair while. It was one of his places, like his workshop, for being alone and having some quiet time to himself. Where the women couldn't get at him and talk.

The day after he'd nailed up the door of the lavatory in the yard she used the indoor one straight after him. She found the curtained casement flung open to let in a stream of sunlight and fresh air. The little room smelled of his pipe tobacco, eau de Cologne, shit. The wooden seat, when she lifted herself on to it, was still warm. She sat there, her feet on tiptoe, just reaching the black and white floor, and gazed at the glazed bumps of the linen towel hanging from a hook on the back of the door, the little wash-basin shaped like a scallop shell, the black and white edging of the tiles above. The cake of violet soap in its tin dish.

Pissing was a tremendous pleasure. Voluptuously abandoning control. Relief as the bursting bladder emptied itself, easing discomfort. Shitting was an equal delight. It was, to begin with, so varied. Some days knobs of shit as hard and beadlike as rabbit droppings fell away from her. Some days slugs or pellets. On others she watched a thick brown snake dive down between her legs. Letting it out felt so good. Shiver as the shit took over, nudged her open, swelled, dropped softly out.

She wiped herself, tossed the paper into the pan, lifted the little button-shaped plunger on the top of the tank. Water swirled into the low wide bowl. In a moment it was empty.

That was what death was like. It rushed upon you and swept you away. Your body became useless, was buried out of sight. Dug into the earth, like compost or manure. Antoinette's soul would go on, everyone promised, but what was it really, the soul? Soon Antoinette would find out whether it was true or not. Léonie picked up the wet cake of soap from the tin dish stencilled with poppies and washed her hands. She left the window open and went downstairs.

THE FRYING-PAN

*A*ntoinette gripped the thread of her life for three more years. During that time Léonie and Madeleine went on coming to France in the school holidays, just as they always had. Louis got thinner, and his hair turned grey. Thérèse began studying for her *baccalauréat*, at the *lycée* in Le Havre. Victorine was more often cross as she raced about with hoovers and dusters and brooms. But the illness at the heart of the house quickly established itself as normal. The way things were. It was hard to feel that much had really changed.

Twenty-five years later, when Thérèse and Léonie at last began to talk to each other about that time, they called it the odd summer. It dragged its feet and whimpered, it crept forward, it flinched. It was a very long summer. It began with both the girls turning thirteen. It was lightened by the presence of Rose Taillé in the house, Rose with her deep voice and her olive skin and her green glass eye.

As Antoinette grew weaker, and left her bed hardly at all, she became frightened to be left alone. It was too gloomy, she said, to lie there all by herself, she wanted to get rid of her depressing thoughts. Madeleine sat with her as much as possible, abandoning her usual household tasks. Victorine brought in Rose to help. Madeleine didn't try to organize the two of them. She let them be.

When you want some extra hands, she told them: get those girls to help.

Almost every day that summer, it seemed to Léonie, there was a hill of beans to prepare, for lunch or dinner. Rose, Victorine, Thérèse and Léonie pulled up chairs to the kitchen table and set to. The thin green beans only needed topping and tailing. Snap crack as your thumbnail bit, then the fresh green smell gushed into the air.

Other sorts of beans had to be shelled like peas, from pods that could be whitish-yellow, or cream speckled with pink. The pods were split and slit with your thumbnail, then the beans thumbed out of the silky inner case. Snugly fitted into it they were flicked out, bulky and milk-white as the pearls from Madeleine's necklace the time it broke and spilt into her plate at lunch. Pearl food. The pearls were fat rice grains you wanted to bite. The pink speckled beans looked like tiny onyx eggs.

When the pierced silver colander on three legs was full you could dig your hands into the beans and trickle their cool slipperiness between your fingers. They might be eaten for supper with a ladleful of thick sourish cream poured over them. Or they might be mixed with onion and garlic softened in butter then stewed with carrots and rosemary to go with roast lamb for lunch.

While their fingers flew in and out of the earthy heap of beans Rose and Victorine talked. They described village life to each other in intricate detail. They passed it back and forth. They crawled across their chosen ground like detectives armed with magnifying glasses. They took any subject and made it manageable. They sucked it and licked it down to size. They chewed at it until, softened, it yielded, like blubber or leather, to their understanding. They went over it repeatedly until it weakened and gave in and became part of them. Tragedy, disaster; they moulded them into small, digestible portions.

They talked, Léonie thought, as freely as though they were alone. She felt invisible and powerful. She stretched and flapped her ears, listened.

Remember how they whitewashed the pigsties before they'd let their men sleep there?

One thing you have to give the Germans, they were very clean.

Very clean, the bastards.

Very polite and correct, that officer, that day.

Those scum of *sales Boches*.

Poor Mademoiselle Antoinette.

Then I found her outside the kitchen door, crying, she'd lost her shoes what with one thing and another and she was too ashamed to come back into the house.

For a long time she wouldn't tell us.

What could we have done?

What else could she have done?

Sssh.

Thérèse, seated opposite Léonie on the other side of the table, was scornful of this kitchen gossip. Oh well, she'd say: I suppose you find it interesting because you're *English*. You're just a visitor after all.

It's different here, Léonie tried to explain: in our kitchen in London no one ever drops in for a chat. There's just the radio.

Thérèse said: I'd rather be reading a book.

But she came to the kitchen when summoned to help, and she tried not to grumble at the repetitive nature of the work and the talk. She said prayers under her breath. For the souls of the dying and the dead. You had to look very cheerful and normal while you worked so that no one would guess you were praying. It was important not to look as though you wanted people to think you were holy. That was a form of spiritual pride.

The problem was that you could never do enough. You could spend your entire life praying for the holy souls, to get them out of purgatory. If, by choosing to suffer a little, by constantly sacrificing your will in small ways, you could rescue souls, then obviously you would be a selfish brute not to. But when did you stop? How could you possibly enjoy yourself if that meant taking time off praying for the holy souls? Offer it up, people said: offer everything up, the happy times too, it's all part of praying for the holy souls.

The two girls sat together at lunch, at the far end of the table. They were allowed to speak to each other in low voices but never to interrupt an adult. The lunch-time conversation tended to be less interesting than that of Rose and Victorine in the kitchen. Further above Léonie's head. She sulked in her white crocheted cardigan and modelled tiny men from the dough of her bread. She slumped in her chair and waited to be told off.

She swore to herself that when she grew up she would not wait so long between courses. She would eat fast if she felt like it. She would put her elbows on the table, she would be allowed wine, she would read a book while she ate if she wanted to. She would eat by candlelight with an orchestra in the corner. She would lay the table her own way, not the French way, and no one would reprove her for putting the forks and spoons face up. She would talk loudly and at length and everyone would have to listen to her or they'd get no food. She would never be ill and she would live to a very old age.

THE PILLOWS

*L*éonie hated the smell in the sickroom. Warm stuffiness, overlaid with eucalyptus, the stabbing odour of disinfectant that couldn't mask that other smell that was Antoinette dying. She kept away. She put her head round the door to say good morning and good night, then ran. Her behaviour was both frowned at and tolerated. Her bad-mannered English side coming out. She wanted to go back to England, to return to school, but she couldn't. Madeleine had taken her away from school. They were staying here.

Thérèse sat by the bed. Antoinette slept with her mouth open, head dropped on to steep pillows. Gasping breaths that said: difficult, difficult. She was restless. Her hands clutched the air and each other, groped for someone who was not there. Or for something whose name Thérèse did not know. Antoinette's legs and feet twitched under the covers, would suddenly throw themselves from side to side. The self-control she exercised when awake was abandoned by her in sleep, her body breaking loose to admit her confusion. Look, I'm dying and I don't know how.

The rope of her orange-grey plait tumbled on to her shoulder. She opened her eyes and looked at Thérèse. Long and considering.

She said: it's so strange.

Then she sank back to her morphine dream. Her fingers plucked at the air until Thérèse reached out and held them in her own. Antoinette wrung her hands inside her daughter's clasp. As soon as Thérèse let go of them they flew apart and fumbled in the air again. Thérèse enclosed them once more and held on. She pulled her mother back. Antoinette opened her eyes again.

A piece of ice to suck, she whispered: that's what I want.

Thérèse held it for her, burning her fingers even as the icy water dripped over them. Soon there was a puddle in the saucer she held under Antoinette's chin. Now her lips looked a little less cracked. Still patched with blisters. They were glossed with ice.

Antoinette smiled.

You are a good girl.

Thérèse stared down at her mother's little clawlike hand. She held it gently: the arm on the end of it was so thin.

Antoinette mumbled: in the cellar, don't let him see, don't let him see me, mustn't catch, safe now?

Her eyes implored. Thérèse squeezed her hand.

You're going off again aren't you, she said: don't worry, I'm here, just let yourself float off to sleep, it's all right.

At supper the food crouched on Thérèse's plate and snarled at her. She pushed her fork into her stuffed tomato then put it down.

I'm not hungry.

If she let it, the food would jump into her mouth and swell her up to grossness. She hated the way her skirts strained at the seams, the way her thighs lolled on her chair, rubbed together when she walked. She hated her stomach which stuck out as though she were pregnant however hard she tried to suck it in. She hated her breasts. Ugly fat cow, she told herself over and over again. It's puppyfat, it's just a phase, Madeleine had hummed to her unhelpfully: I was just like that at your age.

Madeleine said now: I hope you're not going on a diet.

Louis looked up at his daughter.

My little queen's getting to be a lovely big girl. But my goodness, don't girls grow up early these days.

Thérèse stared at the bread knife. She wanted to apply it to her newly grown hips and breasts, to pare off, with quick disgusted flicks of her wrist, the fat that clung to her. She was a slim girl inexplicably encased in walls of fat. She was always hungry. And once she admitted hunger it turned into greed, she was nothing but mouth, teeth, stomach, impossible ever to stop – she was starving. In these moods she could have eaten anything. Sometimes she felt she was crunching up shards of glass, blood all over her mouth. Sometimes she thought that food was like a gag. If she ate enough she would not speak and could not cry out.

Before supper she'd held the bowl while Antoinette threw up. Long yellowish strings like egg yolk. Thérèse had stroked her back with one hand and spoken lovingly. Antoinette had collapsed back on to her pillows. Wrists thinner than a child's. Her knuckles looked so big.

Louis's voice was full of anxiety.

Eat up your supper, my little Thérèse. For my sake.

Thérèse picked up her fork. She polished off her stuffed tomato, held her plate out for more.

THE STATUE
OF THE VIRGIN

Thérèse lay flat on the floor, face down, hands outstretched. She lay in the shape of a cross. As still as possible. Eyelashes tickling the floor, mouth kissing its varnished whorls. She shut her eyes and concentrated on the four last things listed by the catechism: death, judgment, heaven and hell.

Don't let her burn in purgatory, dear God, let her go straight to heaven. Don't let her burn.

Madame Martin, she had heard the doctor tell Madeleine when she listened outside the door: probably only had a week to live. She might go any time.

The priest was summoned. He came wearing his purple confessor's stole and carrying the little box of sacred oils for the anointing of the dying. The bedroom door shut behind him.

But you couldn't be sure that was enough. Just in case, Thérèse performed as many acts of mortification daily as she could think of. Suppose her mother weren't conscious enough to make an Act of Perfect Contrition in the second before she died, well, she'd probably have to go to purgatory for a bit and burn. She, Thérèse, would storm heaven to make sure that didn't happen. So she jumped under the cold shower every morning. She took her coffee black, without sugar. She asked for a second helping of spinach. She allowed herself to read for no more than half an hour a day. When she sat down she didn't let herself rest against the back of the chair. Under her breath, thousands of times a day, she invoked the Holy Name of Jesus.

Clearly she heard the crackling of the flames, saw her mother's flesh scorch and blacken. She shrivelled up, fell forwards, like a paper doll. Cancer was a fire. It ate her mother away.

Thérèse did not possess a hair shirt, or a belt spiked with rusty nails, or a scourge. So she lay on the floor in the shape of a cross, and prayed.

What comforted her, when from time to time she opened her eyes and squinted upwards, was the sight of her statue of Our Lady of Lourdes. The Madonna with a heavenly look, a light veil over her fair hair, blue sash about her girlish waist, hands clasped in ecstasy and a rosary dangling from one arm. Little Bernadette was moulded at the statue's base, by a rosebush in bloom, a stream curling about its foot. A bulky shawl wrapped her head and shoulders and was crossed at her back. She prayed ardently, in rapture. In real life she'd been a poor shepherdess who lived in a dungeon and had asthma. After the visions she'd become a shepherdess of souls, leading them to Our Lady and to repentance. There were no sheep on the Martin farm. Only cows, ducks, rabbits and geese. And they certainly couldn't be called poor, living in this house.

Thérèse groaned at her wandering thoughts. She lifted her head and banged it several times on the floor.

Are you ill? What are you up to? Get up this minute.

The bedroom door was open. Madeleine stood in the doorway. She looked frightened and cross. Her arms were full of freshly ironed towels.

I was tired, Thérèse said: so I was lying down for a bit.

THE CAMP-BED

Madeleine and Victorine carted the camp-bed up the stairs to the second floor, into Thérèse's room. Léonie and Thérèse followed with bedding. They wrestled, all four, to put it up. It dated from the war. Canvas stretched over poles, on metal legs that were jointed like elbows. The poles were pushed in along canvas tunnels at the sides. The difficult bit was getting the short poles at top and bottom to fit into the others. Easy to get your finger trapped in a vicious bite between peg and hole.

There, Madeleine said, gasping: that's it. Wretched thing.

On to the taut canvas base she dumped sheets, two red blankets. She caught Thérèse's eye.

No more trouble. No more ridiculous tricks. Is that clear?

To Léonie she said: no getting up to mischief, d'you hear me?

She marched out, Victorine in tow. Their feet clumped down the stairs.

While Thérèse watched, Léonie hung her few clothes in the wardrobe. She arranged her armful of books on the shelf Thérèse had cleared for her in the corner above the camp-bed. Her diary went under the pillow, her nightdress on top.

Thérèse said: you've been put in here to spy on me. I hate you. I'll never speak to you again.

Léonie considered her nightdress. It was identical to the one Thérèse wore. Both made from remnants of terylene bought by Madeleine at a sale in Le Havre and run up by her on the black and gold sewing-machine you had to pedal like a toy car. Quite a few days it had taken Madeleine, this sewing. She was glad of it. A distraction. Something to do in the long afternoons when the house was clean, empty and hushed, and Antoinette sleeping. She gathered the wrinkly flowered stuff, pink and yellow and blue rosebuds, on to the deep yoke, adding a ruff at the low neckline, pinched the elastic into the edges of the puff sleeves, tramped her needle patiently around the enormous hem. Did this twice. The nighties were big, ankle-length. Room to be grown into, Madeleine said through her mouthful of pins: don't wriggle so, Thérèse.

They were see-through. Madeleine had not considered that. While the girls paraded upstairs, giggling at the glimmer of flesh they showed each other, Madeleine set to again. This time with glossy chintz, large blue roses on a white ground with touches of pink. Peter Pan collars, wide sleeves, blue ribbon ties. Decent. Pretty. Attired in these, the girls could come downstairs to say good night after their bath. Perfectly presentable. No ironing needed, thank God.

Antoinette approved, her blink said. They stood next to her bed and dutifully showed themselves off. But she didn't care any more about Thérèse's clothes. She'd handed over to Madeleine. She drifted off again, back to her private morphine place. Her retreat. Her room next door to death. They kissed her, one cheek each, and departed softly in their pink felt bedroom slippers.

Sitting on the edge of the camp-bed, Léonie considered how to woo Thérèse out of her silence.

Let's have a midnight feast tonight, she said: a secret party. Let's go up on the roof.

Thérèse's head jerked round: how?

To keep themselves awake they sat on the floor and told stories. The grandfather clock in the dining-room sent its notes upstairs every quarter-hour. At half-past eleven the house was so quiet they decided not to wait until midnight.

Léonie chose to use the basket Madeleine carried when she went shopping in the village. Deep, with a strong handle. She filled it from the larder and the fridge. Cold chicken. A bowl of leftover cold veal and rice, its top thick with jelly. A wedge of onion tart. Two peaches. A slice of *bleu d'Auvergne*, another of *Roquefort*. Half a packet of *biscottes*. A litre bottle of wine, glass stars around its neck, that was a third full. If someone had neglected to put it away in the *buffet* after supper, then with luck it had been forgotten and would not be missed.

Thérèse watched. It isn't really stealing, she reassured herself: I live here so I can eat the food. But she didn't believe that. She screwed up her face and whispered: you're so revoltingly fat you disgusting baboon.

Léonie shut the fridge door: right, let's go.

They crept up the back staircase to the third floor, testing each tread for creaks before stepping on it, nightclothes bunched in one hand lest they trip. Inside the first attic, Léonie had discovered, if you fumbled your way through the dusty darkness to what seemed a cupboard on the far side, you found, within this, a ladder clamped to the wall that led to a trapdoor and thence to a bit of flat roof. She went first, plucked the basket from her cousin's lifted arms, then pulled Thérèse up after her.

They sat on the little bit of flat roof above the attic skylight, behind a low parapet. Another ladder behind them led upwards, for the benefit of anyone come to check the steep lift of slates. Below them was the farm, the orchards, the fields. An owl hooted and was answered. Yellow headlights swelled and sank on the road beyond the front gates as a late car swept by. In front of them rode the moon, silver-skirted, in a flurry of dark-blue clouds.

Léonie was too excited to speak. With the penknife from her dressing-gown pocket she sawed the piece of chicken into two portions and handed one to Thérèse. Fingers greasy with lovely chicken fat, mouth attacking the crisp salty skin, the flesh scented with maize and herbs. Thérèse poured a large plastic glassful each of red wine. At supper, now they were thirteen, they were allowed one tumbler, well watered. Neat, the wine made them choke. They gasped and sat back, determined to like it. They made sandwiches of Roquefort and sliced peach. The cold veal, meat jelly and rice, scooped up with their fingers, was one of the best things, they agreed, they'd ever eaten. Léonie licked Thérèse's fingers to see if they tasted the same as her own. They chucked the peach stones over the parapet so that peach trees would grow in the garden next year and surprise everyone.

Now the night was cool. They'd been sitting still for too long. The stars sprang out, pressed themselves at their faces, as a wind blew up and chased away the clouds below the moon. So bright, so indifferent, that moon. Inside herself, as she looked at it, Thérèse felt sour and queer.

She whispered: I want to go back in.

Léonie climbed into bed beside her.

Where does it hurt?

Thérèse pointed at her stomach, lay back. Léonie's hand rubbed up and down, kneaded, caressed. Smooth strokes along the cool skin. Her hand had a mouth and could talk. Be still, I'll take care of you.

Thérèse sat up and fumbled for the light-switch that dangled from a cord beside the bed. She brought her fingers up from under the sheets and stared at them. Bright red.

She said: it must be what they told us about. That thing women get. When you can't go swimming.

Léonie was awed. The blood was thin and clear. A lot of it. Trust Thérèse to get hers first. It wasn't fair.

She scrambled out of bed.

Wait there, I'll go and fetch someone.

Thérèse sounded frightened.

Hurry up then.

Madeleine's room was empty. There was a light under Antoinette's door. Léonie peered in. Antoinette seemed to be asleep. Louis and Madeleine were slumped on the sofa by the fireplace. Louis dozed, his head on Madeleine's shoulder. Her deepset eyes stared in front of her as though she was thinking of somewhere far away.

THE COFFEE BOWLS

*L*ouis looked as though he'd just got up off the ground after being knocked out in a fight. Grief had swung at him and given him two red eyes. He sagged inside his best grey suit, and his black armband looked like a bandage. He had two fresh shaving scars on his chin which his fingers kept wandering up to touch. The suit removed him from what they were all trying to pretend was a normal breakfast. Léonie, used to him clad in blue jacket and brown corduroy trousers, didn't feel able to kiss him good morning. He didn't notice her lack of salute. He stared at the tablecloth while Madeleine poured coffee into his big cup. This morning he didn't dip his bread and butter into it, munch and gulp, as usual. He just stared at the tablecloth. Léonie tucked herself into a chair at the far end of the table, next to the silent Thérèse, who wasn't eating either. She broke off a piece of *baguette*, spread it with butter and jam, stuffed it into her mouth.

Victorine, Rose and Madeleine were all in black. They stood over Louis.

All right then? It's time to go. The cars have arrived.

Thérèse and Léonie watched them depart. They crouched on the windowseat of the little white *salon*, face pressed against the cold glass, misting it. Louis, walking out to the long black car, was a sack of tears. You could see he'd stuck invisible tape over his mouth so as not to cry. He had forbidden the two girls to attend the Requiem Mass because he said it would upset them too much.

The two black cars pulled out of the gates, round the corner, and were gone. Léonie and Thérèse knelt down on the parquet floor. Eyes shut, hands clasped. They recited the *De Profundis* together, dividing the lines between them. Out of the depths have I cried to thee O Lord.

Lord, hear my voice. And let thine ears be attentive. To the voice of my supplication. If thou O Lord shalt observe iniquities. Lord who shall endure it?

They couldn't remember any more. They left it there, and went back to the breakfast table, to their unfinished bowls of *café au lait.* The coffee was cold, with skin on it.

Léonie was bursting with English words. She ran upstairs to the bathroom, covered her head with a towel and spoke to the cold white wall.

I'm glad she's dead. She had to die. She took too long dying. I'm glad she's dead.

The house was very still. It listened to her. It was making up its mind what to reply. The bath-towel over her head was warm and dry on her face. She leaned her ear against the wall.

THE BREAD-BASKET

Thérèse no longer shared the first job of the day with her cousin. Léonie went alone, now, to fetch the bread from the baker's in the village square. On her return she laid the cloth, collected the knives and plates, sounded the gong for breakfast. Thérèse was let off these tasks because she was in mourning. She slumped in bed, miserable and full of headache.

Poor child, Madeleine said: no wonder.

Thérèse had not once cried in public for her mother. Louis wept openly and could not be comforted. Not with caresses, not with sweets.

Leave him be, for the moment, Madeleine advised: leave him alone and he'll be all right.

Two days since the funeral. Léonie was delighted to get out of the house. She shut the kitchen door behind her, turned to study the strip of seaweed nailed there, to check the weather. It suggested wet. It was right. As she emerged into the yard fine rain dampened her face. The air smelled of salt and the sky was grey.

She sauntered around the side of the house, hands in the pockets of her shorts, trod over the white gravel to the gates. She heard a thin crowing of cocks. Her bare feet slipped in her sandals, which were already wet, and her cotton shirt felt chilly. Too much bother to fetch a raincoat. She went on out to the main road.

The ditch on her left swirled with rainwater. The bank above it was a tangled slope of late-flowering mallow and campion, bright purple-pink in the long grass. On her right the green meadow was full of cows. Every so often there was a gap in the bank of beech trees that guarded the farm from wind and storms, a muddy track between red brick gateposts affording entry for tractors into the farm lands, access to the half-timbered cottages where the farm workers and their families lived. Already the labourers' wives were returning from the village, long loaves tucked under their arms. Some rode ancient and solid bicycles. Others trudged along in wellingtons, a bulging canvas bag in each hand. Léonie knew them all by sight. She greeted each one.

The road wound away from the Martin farm into the outskirts of the village. Léonie plodded between small houses that leaned together. Through their open doors she caught flashes of patterned lino floor, a corner of tablecloth, a chair leg. Voices inside called out, responded. She went on, past the blacksmith's, past the corrugated-iron public lavatory on the corner, plastered with faded posters that peeled and flapped, across the road, through the stepped gap between two old houses whose lath and plaster upper storeys almost touched overhead, and into the little square.

She walked very slowly across it. She told herself she would not be shy, she would not blush when addressed as *la petite Anglaise*, she would not mind having her fluency admiringly remarked upon, she would not care that everyone in the shop would turn round and stare at her, the foreigner. Today would be different.

The two bakeries stood side by side. Almost identical, if you had not been brought up by Victorine to know that one was good and the other bad: both had wide shop windows displaying shelves of apple tarts, turnovers, puffs; striped awnings above; tiled steps.

Léonie stared at the two shops and came to a decision. She would go into the bad woman's shop. The collaborator's shop. Just to see what it was like. Surely nobody at home would notice if the bread, just once, tasted a bit different?

She pushed open the glass door, muttered good morning, and took her place in the queue. She couldn't believe that she wasn't in the baker's next door. Same list of icecream flavours hung on the wall and bowl of aniseed lollipops on the counter, same gilt baskets of *croissants* and racks like umbrella stands packed with tall loaves. The woman in the grey overall serving customers looked just like anyone else. She snatched up a square of tissue paper, deftly swung and twisted it round a fat *brioche*.

Léonie bought two *baguettes*. The shop-woman smiled at her and asked after the bereaved family. Léonie felt her cheeks go red. She gabbled something polite and slunk out of the door, just remembering in time to bid everybody goodbye.

She slung her long loaves over her shoulder, a bread rifle, cupping its warm heel in her joined palms. She turned towards the shallow stone steps leading out of the square.

Baptiste, four other boys behind him, blocked her path. Sweat flowed from Léonie's armpits down to her waist.

Eengleesh peeg, Baptiste yelled at her.

The boys whistled. Léonie wheeled, scrambled back past the baker's, and fled along the boulevard edged with limes that led to the church and the walled cemetery, to the lane beyond.

The boys jeered as she ran away. She let herself glance back. They'd vanished. And she still had the bread, clutched in her arms. Fear fell off her like a jacket. Her heartbeat slackened.

The drizzle had stopped. Sun shone on water. She slithered along the muddy ruts of the overgrown lane. Getting her sandals filthy but she didn't care. Delicious, the coolness of mud between her toes. Brambles hooked her shorts, unloaded raindrops all over her feet. Ferns of brilliant green slapped her legs. She picked one, hoisting the bread under one arm, and swished it over her shoulder at the swarm of cattle flies that buzzed there.

The lane was deserted, quiet. She remembered Victorine saying hardly anyone used it any more. It was a much longer way back than the road. She would be late, even if she stopped dawdling and got a move on. Her pace slowed even more as she thought of the house dark and sour with grief. And it would be her fault that breakfast would be late. She'd get a scolding from Victorine and from Madeleine as well most likely.

The strap of one of her sandals had worked itself loose. She stopped, shook her foot experimentally. The sandal flew off. At the same moment Baptiste and his gang of boys ran whooping round the corner.

Boys behind, the woods in front. Léonie pelted down the lane, scattering loaves. Freed of her burden she was fleet. She leapt over the ditch opposite the Martins' orchard wall and hurled herself into the undergrowth. The woods received her, closed over and around her, dense green water.

They hadn't followed her in. Jeering laughter, then their voices faded. Léonie sat up, rubbing her elbows. Her legs were scratched and smarting. Her foot, when she explored it with her fingers, had a couple of thorns stuck in it and was bleeding. Now she'd be in extra trouble for losing the sandal. And the bread. Did she dare go back to look for it? Suppose the boys were hiding, waiting for her to re-emerge?

She got up and limped forward. She was in a little clearing, in the centre of which was a tall heap of large stones. Behind it was a small white cliff, the bubble of water. She paused. Memory of a basket to be filled with blackberries. Victorine's tale of . . . she couldn't quite remember what.

She stood and shivered. It had begun to rain again. She hovered, not knowing what to do, afraid to start crying here all by herself.

Something like a rough finger stroked the back of her neck. Her head jerked up. Then she saw it. Saw the fine rainy air become solid and golden and red, form itself into the shape of a living and breathing woman.

Later, when she blurted out to Victorine what she had seen, when she tried to describe it, she struggled with inadequate words. Under Victorine's mocking questioning she understood that she had betrayed her vision by mentioning it. Its red and gold brilliance sank into the darkness of her imagination like a firework blazing then fading in the black night sky. All she had left to clutch at was the memory of how she had felt.

Something outside her, mysterious and huge, put out a kindly exploring hand and touched her. Something was restored to her which she had lost and believed she would never find again. The deepest pleasure she had ever known possessed her. It started in her toes and across her shoulders and squirmed through her, aching, sweet.

Then she remembered it. A language she once knew but had forgotten about, forgotten ever hearing, forgotten she could speak. Deeper than English or French; not foreign; her own. She had heard it spoken long ago. She heard it now, at first far off, thin gold, then close, warm. The secret language, the underground stream that forced through her like a river, that rose and danced inside her like the pulling jet of a fountain, that wetted her face and hands like fine spray, that joined her back to what she had lost, to something she had once intimately known, that she could hardly believe would always be there as it was now, which waited for her and called her by her name.

Time stilled, and suspended itself. In the cool drizzle. Then, with a jerk, the world went on again.

Victorine and the others were interested solely in what she claimed to have seen. Léonie tried to tell them. It came out all confused.